Chronicles of De
Volume

The Moon
Is Made Of
Custard

Chronicles of Dennis Foster
Volume I

The Moon
Is Made Of
Custard

Dick Wolsey

A Cardinal Classics edition first published by Old Forge Studio 2024

ISBN 978-1-0687398-0-4 paperback

ISBN 978-1-0687398-1-1 hardback

ISBN 978-1-0687398-2-8 epub

All illustrations by and © Dick Wolsey

Typeset by www.shakspeareeditorial.org

Dedicated to

Rebecca Bryony & Eleanor Victoria
Bedtime reading to you both as children was an honour and a
delight. This story is for you.

Jay Beales (CF sufferer) 1984 to 2021
My dearest friend Jay may no longer be amongst us, but his
undeniable quirky humour and lust for life helped me reflect on
life's fragility and what becomes of us at the end. He would have
loved a ride in the telephone box.

Contents

Playlist

Whilst writing The *Moon is Made of Custard*, I enjoyed the company of numerous songs and instrumental pieces. A number of tracks particularly resonated with the rhythm of the story. Tones, melodies, characters and distant worlds fused harmoniously with my crazy narrative.

I hope you connect to these tracks as I did whilst reading *The Moon is Made of Custard*.

Chapter	Title/Artist	Chapter	Title/Artist
1	*Revilo* Steph Strings	11	*Bad* Royal Deluxe
2	*Reaper* Silverberg, Jordan Frye	12	*In The Hall Of The Mountain King* London Symphony Orchestra
3	*Mombasa* Two Cellos	13	*A Girl Like You* Edwyn Collins
4	*True Colors* Cindy Lauper	14	*Time In A Bottle* Jim Croce
5	*A Million Dreams* Pink	15	*Wherever You Will Go* The Calling
6	*I Don't Remember* Peter Gabriel	16	*Bitch* Meredith Brooks
7	*Firework* Katy Perry	17	*Lost In Space* Lighthouse Family
8	*This Is Me* Keala Settle	18	*A Thousand Years* Christina Perri
9	*Rocket Man* Elton John	19	*If* Bread
10	*You've Got A Friend* James Taylor	20	*'O Fortuna' Carmina Burana* Carl Orff
		Epilogue	*Here, There And Everywhere* The Beatles

Listen on Spotify: https://open.spotify.com/playlist/6EswFTLb5WeG4hrh9gNgLV.

1. Ctrl-Alt-Del

I was tired of being in this soulless office. Tired of this half-baked cleaning job and tired of most things actually. So why did my life seem so vacant, without purpose, forward or backwards? To be honest, I felt abandoned, always had, and tonight beneath heavy skies, I was again fed up with being stuck in the fug of nowhere.

Rain plip plopped down the window, as though it couldn't be bothered. Slumped across the desk, thumbing through a heap of dull brochures, I knew watching paint dry would be far more interesting.

I'd piled brushes, mop, rags, and other cleaning stuff by the door, and a bucket of dirty water waited patiently to be thrown out. At some point I'd head off, having cleaned the office, but getting motivated this late was difficult. As it was, purpose in my life had never been a thing.

Even the plip plops buggered off, they were so bored, but the silence was momentary, as sheets of rain unexpectedly pounded the window. To be honest, I should have locked up when I had the chance, got to the car and sodded off home. But as rivers ran down the glass, there was no way I was getting soaked.

Sighing heavily, I returned to thumbing pages. Delightful cottages, parcels of woodland and expensive properties screamed 'BUY ME.' However, their lavish cause was lost on me, rain or not.

Boredom, pure and simple, caused the longest of yawns. What fun could there possibly be in dealing with overpriced bunkum every day, sucking up to clients whilst emptying their bank accounts like quicksand? I'm sure smiles had been invented for something more worthy. As if I knew. Yet whatever I thought about their monotonous, buy-one-sell-one world, it was a damn sight more exciting than mine – but only just.

Without warning, the desktop burst into life. Images scrolled and flashed across the screen, yet the frustration of seeing what I could never afford provoked a sense of resentment.

I arched my back, rolled my shoulders, and stretched towards the window as another yawn rolled into the room without care or interest. A tsunami of rain washed chaotically over the gutters and down the pane. There was no point in going home just yet. Marvellous.

As I mulled over the distinct lack of options, a brilliant flash of lightning and clap of thunder shook me and the building. All the lights failed, and the PC went off, whilst the ringing in my ears played merrily on. For a few dazed seconds, I wondered what to do. But as expected, nothing came to mind. So, there I was, bound to wait out the bloody storm. The upside? At least I was in the dry.

It mattered not how long I stayed in the building; no-one would care, and no-one would miss me. Such was the life of a dull bachelor in a dull village on the outskirts of Who Gives A Shit City. Why did everything seem to conspire against me? I had no idea. It wasn't for lack of asking for help; it just never came. Perhaps I was programmed like this, or maybe I needed someone to give me a push. Who knows; I didn't.

The lights flashed on for a moment, but not much else. As the darkness continued, I guessed nothing was broken, so nothing to fix. Likewise, there was no point looking for candles or a torch, for I knew as soon as I found them the power would come back on. That was Sod's Law and summed up my worth nicely.

Within the gloom, the warm office quickly faded, and my breath floated like early morning mist. The cold didn't deter me, as I swung my ragged trainers up onto the desk, shuffled into the soft seat and pulled my hoodie up around me. My head dropped back into my hands, and I closed my eyes. Ahhh, that was better.

Listening to the rhythm of the beating rain, I began counting wet sheep, whilst a deep yawn, and then another, told me bed would soon be calling. Thunder and lightning danced up above, shake, rattle and rolling the little building and me, just south of nowhere.

How long I'd been asleep I didn't know, but in my slumber, gravity seemed to have won the race. In the darkness, I peeled myself from the carpet and looked across at the office clock. The tick-tock was eerily silent from when I last looked over. It seemed to have stopped and so had my watch. Of course it was the storm; what else could have stopped both devices? Death, perhaps? I chuckled nervously. What an idiot.

From out of the gloom, the desktop flashed into life and a bright white spot stared at me from the centre of the screen. I blinked and squinted, mesmerised at first. But when nothing else happened, I whacked the screen.

'Come on, you piece of …'

Before I could say what I felt, the spot vanished, and the gloom returned. Irrespective of the outcome of the storm, it was clear there was little to be done, so I felt compelled to lock up and get bloody soaked after all.

No alarms showed on the fire panel, nor faults on the security system, so in my tired mind things were good. Anyway, I'd leave the morning team a note about the storm. However, as I turned to head out, the damned PC lit up again. This time light flooded the room.

'Are you kidding?'

Such was the intensity of the light, I couldn't just walk away. OCD wouldn't let me. As I stretched across to the power button, there in the centre of the screen, a bizarre message appeared:

BE CAREFUL WHAT YOU WISH FOR

Clever things, these computers, but not always the friendliest. My finger lingered just short of the button as I stared at the message. Then another appeared:

GO HOME…GO NOW!

That spooked the dullness out of me, I can say.

Tired I might be, but now I was irritated. So, rather than doing what I'd intended, I did the opposite. I'd show who was boss, and I pushed the power button, hard.

And again.

But the screen stayed on. Of course it did!

I stabbed the button repeatedly, so much so that had it been a person, blood would have spilled. The screen scowled back. No, I wasn't going to be defeated, nope, not me, so I pummelled the Esc key and Ctrl-Alt-Del over and over. Nothing changed.

Yanking the plug from the extension lead would end our battle of wits for certain, but no, that didn't work. It still scowled for all its worth. Out of frustration, I punched the power button and keyboard. And there it was, an idiot without any finger on any pulse, in a dull world they couldn't control. Bloody marvellous!

Just then, a blinding light flashed through the office window and my arm rose instinctively to shield my face. The room was awash in light – not white light, but purples, reds, and oranges. As they danced and swirled around me, a warmth enveloped my feet and ankles. Perhaps the heating had switched back on. Perhaps I was in a trance. Or, more likely, I'd peed myself.

However, as the light intensified, the warmth beneath dropped like a stone; cool, cold, and colder still. I went to step away from the fierce light but couldn't; my feet were anchored fast. Then my lungs went on strike, and my chest locked up tight. I was having a heart attack. What else could it be?

So these were my final moments, in a dull office, in a dull street, just north of nothing. Shit, what were the chances? However, in that moment, three things happened.

First, something solid slammed heavily into the side door, making me jump.

In the next instant, someone grabbed my hand, hauling me off my feet.

And finally, a cold voice demanded, 'Hurry. Follow me!'

I had no choice in the matter and thankfully nor did my lungs.

All I could see were my dirty old trainers following me through the air, past desk, chair, umbrella rack and cleaning stuff. At the same time, the searing light outside moved toward the large office window. As my head reached the side door, the cab of an enormous truck smashed through the window, towards the desk and all it lovingly possessed.

As I passed through the door, I saw myself at the desk, finger pushing the power button. What was I thinking? All I'd had to do was go home, not turn it off or try to fix it. No, not me, I couldn't even do that. So I was dull and stupid one moment and would be a very dead dimwit the next.

The small office exploded on impact and that was the last I saw of me; stupid old me, standing without wit, behind a desk, in a pokey old estate agents, doing a job I had no care about.

Glass, bricks, glossy brochures, and the contents of the cleaning bucket radiated outward in slow motion. I fell not onto the doorstep or tarmac outside – that would have been too bloody simple. Oh no, I just fell…and fell…and fell, like flippin' Alice.

The darkness of nothing is frighteningly dark. No top notes of dullness there. Yet as I fell, my hand was still firmly gripped. Toward what or where I was headed, I didn't know, but for once in my dull life I *did* care.

2. Treacle-Legged

Down I fell, without knowing who on earth was beside me. Into the unknown we plummeted, without updraft or turbulence, yet I sensed we weren't totally out of control. However, for all I knew, we could be plunging headfirst into oblivion.

Thunder snapped around my heels in the darkness. The office door was now but a pin prick of light behind, but as I looked back, I sensed dread deep in my bones. In the void, an ominous dark figure floated in and out of the beam of light.

Scared? For Christ's sake, I couldn't hold it in and screamed into the inky nothingness, 'There's something behind!'

'No need to shout. I can see them.' The grip relaxed momentarily.

Then THUD. I'd stopped in an instant on my feet, upright without pain or obvious injury. I looked up nervously. Yep, the figure was growing ever larger, and what was that? A bloody sword or something? As far as my frazzled brain cared, it neither wanted to know nor find out.

'This way!' It wasn't a request.

Once more I was being pulled hard, running in utter darkness on an unknown surface, in an unknown direction, to God knows where. The more I ran the more frightened I became. Deep down, I knew there was no going back.

Strange shapes, things cold and wet, brushed my face and body; each time sparks flickered and crackled like static. This way and that we went, and to be fair I wasn't much help, being dragged like a ragdoll. I banged and crashed into mysterious things. Even yelps broke into the inkiness around me. Terrified? They didn't make pants big enough to hold in the terror I was feeling right now.

I looked to my legs but couldn't see them. All I knew was they were running the best they could through what felt like thick treacle. In this crazy dream, I was desperate to speed up – who wouldn't want to? Except I couldn't. Drenched in the horror of it all, I prayed to wake up, for it all to go away. Neither happened.

As we darted this way and that, my mysterious partner heaved me onward. They didn't care about my legs until they said, 'Faster, much faster!' I didn't need that sort of encouragement.

I was desperately doing as I was told, but I couldn't go faster. Treacle's not thin air. It's bloody treacle in every language. My heart pounded like it was insane and dread was clawing its way out of my aching chest. Fight? I had nothing in me, and flight was right there up its arse. You treacle-legged useless twat!

Whether we went faster or not I couldn't tell but with every step I felt worse. Even though I knew I should, I couldn't face the horror behind. The hairs on my neck and arms seemed more than happy to see what was coming. Each strand told me to run faster, much faster. The little shits.

Then, from out of nowhere, off to the right, a bright shop window emerged through the mist. In an instant, there I stood in front of the window, gasping for breath. My legs were exhausted and felt as though they lagged miles behind. And then, plip, plop.

Oh great. Anyone got an umbrella? No, thought not.

In those crazy moments, I tried my utmost to understand what the hell was going on, but that scrambled head of mine couldn't fathom jack shit. With a mind full of mush, I peered through the grubby glazing. All I could see was an array of broken TV screens, differing shapes, sizes, and stacked precariously one upon the other. Aerials bent and broken made the display seem like a giant hedgehog, and the old torn curtains, cobwebs and dust proved it was a place long forgotten.

Grotesque veins of scarlet rain dribbled without care down the windows and pooled beneath me as my head spun in chaos. Something bad was coming, I could smell it, and being brave wasn't an option; I was way past that.

Though they'd long since worked, I sensed somehow the TVs knew I was there. In the centre of the display, a small one flickered on, as if it had been waiting for me. There I stood, exhausted, head down, heart pounding, as I drank in air as quick as I could. It was impossible to tell how I felt; far too many questions poured into the normally empty space between my ears. What now? What's that behind? Where am I? What's going on?

Questions without any obvious hope of answers didn't help, and standing soaked in a deepening pool of blood, in front of a stupid window, meant nothing to me. Why should it, being on the verge of losing it totally and all that. Yet whilst I might have momentarily forgotten my unknown assistant in all of this yahoo, they hadn't forgotten me.

Before I had time for another desperate thought, I was pushed forward off my feet. Oh, here we go again! I flew toward the display, screeching in a way that would terrify the elderly at fifty paces. I had no time to shield my face, close my eyes or stick my head up my arse and kiss my life goodbye.

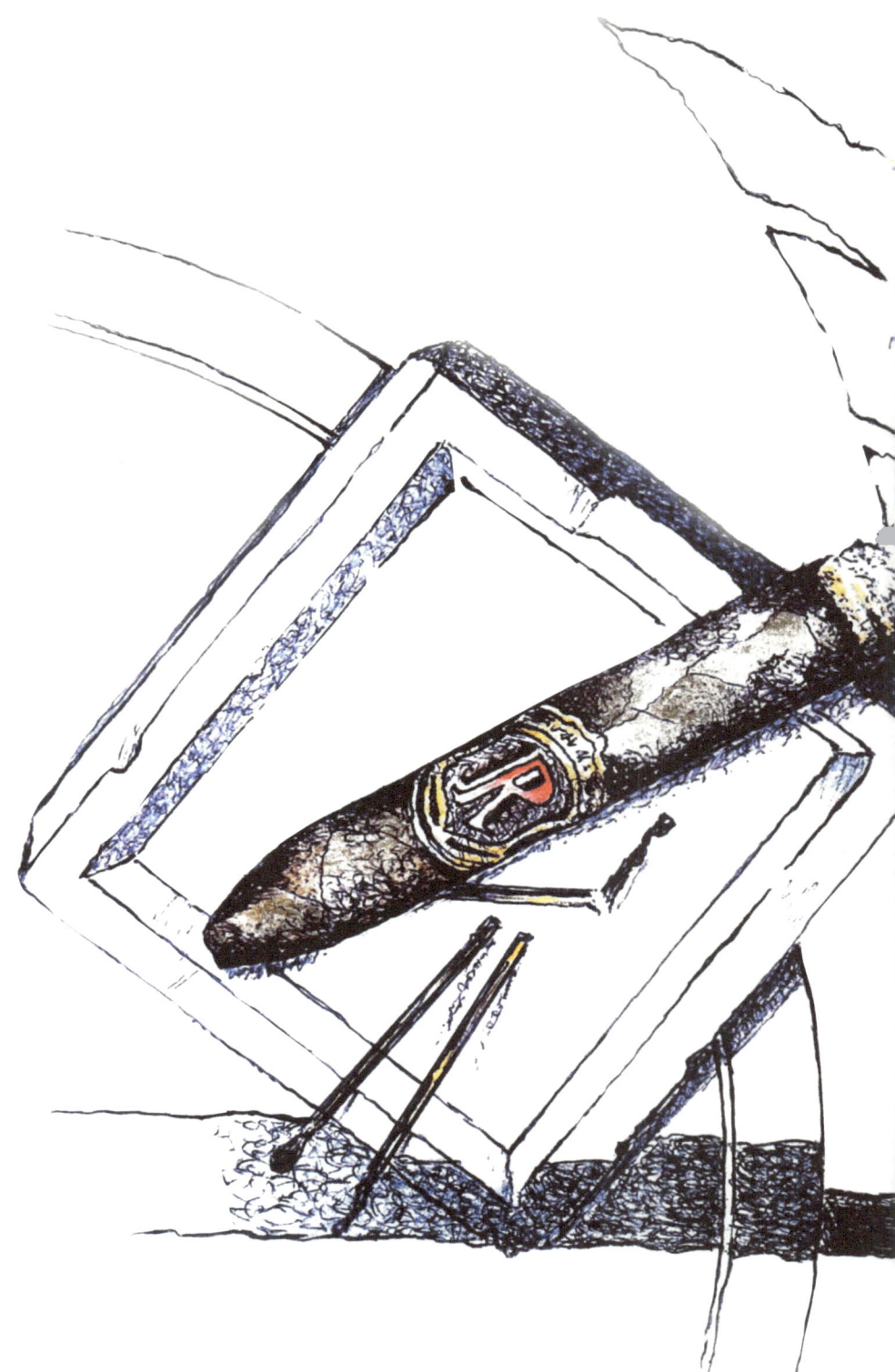

3. Exit Stage Left

Those moments I thought were my last, and at any other time I would have filled my pants. It was more luck than judgement – I hadn't eaten for a while, and thank Christ I hadn't, for kebab looks bad enough the first time around.

However, impact and broken glass never came. Oh boy, this was nuts, I just kept going, through the window, ploughing into the middle TV screen itself. Just sucked into the damned thing. And what was being shown on the screen? I don't know, some old black-and-white drama. What did it matter?

Yet in another instant, onto a large theatre stage I rolled, till exhausted upon some dusty old boards, I stopped.

Beside me, moments later, another figure, dripping wet, landed heavily on top of me. In that missionary fashion, we looked at each other for a couple of seconds, her down, me up.

In my panic, I pushed her off like she had the plague.

Twice over she tumbled before face planting in the dust. The look of surprise on her face said it all.

'Ohhh, no need to thank me.' She coughed and rose to her feet, brushing herself down with obvious resentment.

My eyes followed but not my body.

She twizzled around on the stage, splattering red rainwater like Death's own garden sprinkler. 'Get up, you twit, we need to get going!'

And with that, an almighty cheer came from a vast, unseen crowd behind us. We both turned and peered into the auditorial gloom. Theatre patrons stood out of their seats, clearly enjoying the marvel of two weirdos dropping into some la-di-da theatre production.

Drama, it seemed, had suddenly turned to farce.

The woman's wet hand pulled me to my feet.

As I took in the surroundings, I saw a cast of lesbians glaring, pointing accusing fingers at me.

'I haven't a clue what's going on,' was all I could say, and to that not-unreasonable comment, howls of laughter and more cheering burst from the audience.

'Bravo, bravo,' they cried.

But not the cast dressed in period garments. They appeared well glum and rather pissed off.

My partner turned her gaze toward me. 'I know what you're thinking, Dennis.'

'I very much doubt that. Where the hell are we? And who the hell is Dennis?'

'Firstly, I don't have the plague. Secondly, it's pronounced *thespian*. Thirdly, you've completely torn the arse out of your trousers and they're loving it. And, last but not least, that's your name!'

The nonsense of her response made me scowl and grimace almost simultaneously. She hadn't helped one bit, so I happily returned to scowling as hands raced to cover my blushing backside. Even the cast started to slow clap, probably hoping the intruders would bugger off and they could return the house to normality.

'Exit stage left,' she ordered, as I headed right.

'But my name *isn't* Dennis.'

Off the stage we ran, through the wings, along corridors, up steps and down again, past stagehands, weird props, fusty clothing rails and dim lighting.

It went on…and on…and on…and on.

This was a dream bordering on nightmare, for as hard as we

tried, we just couldn't get out of the building.

'In here,' she ordered.

We barged through yet another door, but this time the broken Stage Manager sign denoted a place of purpose. Oh really? Step by step, my head was amassing questions exponentially and I already had a million or so lined up. As my chest heaved for breath, I knew I wouldn't be asking for answers anytime soon.

My partner slammed the door behind us, slid three rusty bolts across and stood looking around the room. It was typically full of faded theatrical artifacts, coffee-stained newspaper clippings, make-up, wigs, and a rickety desk in front of a mangy old curtain. A half-smoked cigar still smouldered in an ashtray.

She stomped forward, pulled back the desk and the curtain to reveal…nothing of any use, I suspected.

But she turned, looking pleased with herself.

'Just as I thought, and just what we need. I have a nose for these things!'

I peered around her. There lurked another door, pint sized, fixed horizontally. I had no idea what we needed or what she had planned, but she seemed pleased enough as she scurried around muttering.

I didn't share her enthusiasm. Worry is always worry…isn't it?

In amongst my ever-expanding list of questions, I could only think to ask a really stupid one. 'Whoever uses that, the cat?'

Her reply surprised me, yet at the same time unnerved the hell out of me. 'Good question, Dennis. Something that doesn't walk like you and me. More a case of what uses it than who, though. Want to find out?'

Before I could say 'not really', she pulled me to the back of the smelly room. I'd no chance to discuss the ins and outs of why I was now standing across the room, facing the stupidly small doorway.

Unexpectedly, my mind whistled back to an earlier point I was having trouble shaking. Who the *hell* was this Dennis chap? There was just no way that was me. No, it wasn't, it couldn't be. That wasn't me, I was…er, I was…

'OWW! What the heck?'

Cuffing me around the ear brought me quickly back to *wherever* the hell we were, and scowling was becoming a default condition. We looked at each other; she expectantly, and…suddenly her proposal clicked.

'Keep your scowl on the doorway, not me,' she barked.

'For goodness' sake, I can't get through that teeny-weeny door. Have you seen the size of me, or of you? It would be a squeeze for a baby!'

'Two things to remember before I ever get chance to answer all your bloody questions. One, we're being hunted! And two, who gives a shit, get through the door before I push you again.'

You know when you were scolded by the teacher at school, making you feel stupid? Well, this wasn't one of those moments, but it should have been. However, fortitude came bowling through me like gas.

'Well, I've been through a TV already, so here I go,' I said, and ran at the opening.

I didn't hear her cry, 'Not yet, Dennis.'

I smacked hard into the wall and dropped like a stone into the grime of years. I spluttered and coughed dust like talcum powder. 'Bloody hell!'

'Let me open it first, you nit.' And with that, she gently pulled the handle.

The door dropped down, barely missing my head, to reveal a snow-covered mountain landscape.

'Go on then, hurry! He's not far behind us.'

At that, the door to the room shook, as did everything else. The cigar dropped to the floor and ancient dust rained down from above. That was no theatre manager, and as the sliding bolts began moving from their keep, we looked at each other. You could sum up everything about our plight and our reaction in one word: panic!

She was mortified.

I was terrified. 'For Pete's sake, woman,' was all I had time to declare before she pulled me once again to the back wall.

I closed my eyes and leapt across to where I hoped the small opening would be, expecting bruising at the very least.

Miraculously, I landed in the middle of a snow-covered, hilly meadow sort of place. Again, my companion dropped in, but I was quicker this time and she face-planted heavily in the snow, much to my delight. She coughed, spluttered and spat as melting snow dribbled down her cheeks.

'Did you lock the door?' I asked, not knowing why that would make any difference to our frightening predicament.

'Of course! And I've added a few extra locks for good measure. Unfortunately, it won't hold him off for long.'

Wiping her wet and now dirty face, she peered this way and that, seemingly getting her bearings or perhaps thinking to call for a very fast taxi.

I didn't have to think too deeply about my next question.

'Why are we running?'

'It's a long story, but it does have a happy beginning.'

That threw me. 'Happy beginning?'

'Yep. Haven't quite got to the end yet, Dennis. And before you ask, that's why I'm here.'

She smiled that smug sort of smile. One you don't know whether it's trapped wind or something worse, the truth.

'Can I assume this will have a happy end?'

She didn't reply, so I continued.

'So, as I sit on cold, wet snow in some godforsaken alpine pasture, lost, hungry and being chased by Christ knows what, I'd be more inclined to think I'd been hit by an enormous lorry, and this was the fun part of dying!'

My face was screwed tight in frustration, foreseeing what annoying comment she was going to make – '*Well, for one thing…*'

But she didn't.

What she said was much worse.

4. Fragments of Bratwurst

'You're kind of dead, and still could be if Reaper gets his claws on your soul. But it's my job to keep you from him. Does that make sense?'

My mind was on the cusp of nonsense and although I didn't know it at the time, I was running for my life or maybe hurtling toward my death. Anyhow, I exploded in a volatile mix of utter frustration and fear!

'For fuck's sake, woman, can you hear yourself? Is this for real? I'm being rescued, *possibly*. Is that it? Are you some sort of SAS angel? Are you?'

With a face that probably looked like Munch's Scream, I was certain she knew I hadn't grasped what all this meant. I never got to ask who Reaper was, yet she tried her best to help, I think.

'Just consider for a moment being dead, being alive, and then being somewhere in between, in a dream, so to speak. That's where you are.'

Before I could say, 'You are fucking kidding', I should have anticipated that my accomplice would do what she did. I doubted she planned to spend eternity answering my million or so questions, so a fair chunk of snow slammed into my jaw.

I turned my ice-splattered face away, bracing for the next snowball. It didn't come; nor did I think to throw one back, but I should've. A sudden shiver rattled my cooling bones. I cautiously opened one eye and lowered my hand. She'd disappeared. I spun around, but she wasn't in sight, not a single footprint either. She'd buggered right off and, to be honest, I was good with that. Whilst my shoulders relaxed, the shivering increased.

'Oi, Dennis, you menace, over here.'

For someone whose name wasn't Dennis, I felt strangely antagonised, but I was starting to recognise its relationship with yours truly. It just didn't sound right. I spun around, looking for her somewhere, anywhere, just so I could give her the satisfaction that she'd pissed me off. She was still nowhere to be seen. Then an almighty pile of snow dropped from above.

'Oh, sod off, will you!' I spluttered through a mouth of ice. The shivering thought it was hilarious and doubled its efforts to shake my body to pieces.

'I thought you'd be happier knowing you weren't dead, not quite dead, but it seems you're not happy at all, Mr Grumpy Bum.'

Shivering in the cold snow, I looked annoyingly at the little she-devil hovering above me, her legs and arms casually folded. She was grinning. I wasn't.

'If, Dennis,' she began, 'you were dead, I can guarantee you'd not be having this much fun in the snow. *If* you were dead, I can guarantee you'd not be having *any* fun.' She giggled. 'If you want to live, then you must understand a few things, and crucially, must do as I say or ask or tell you. If you're dissatisfied with this gold buffet service and you don't want to live, then I'll happily unlock the last door and see what comes through. Make no mistake, he's not after me.'

A different shiver went through me, not of cold, but one of dread. I was exhausted, and she had a fair point.

'I'm too cold to argue, but isn't this just a dream or some ridiculous nightmare? Won't I wake up and everything will be back to how it was?'

'That's a few questions, and to be fair they have merit. But no, you won't wake up, for you're not asleep, and yet you are. Hmmm, difficult to understand, I know, but you'll figure it out. And yes, it feels nightmarish but it's that last bit that worries me.'

I'd already forgotten.

She sighed.

'You want to return to being the dullard you've always whined about being? Seriously? Well, spoiler alert, you're almost dead, a door away from oblivion, and you would like to go back to being worse than dead! You're not dull, Dennis Foster, you've just never lived. To be honest, I think I'd get more thanks from a slug!'

Slug? I ignored that last bit.

We seemed to be getting nowhere fast in this cold wonderland. 'Dennis Foster? Never heard of him. I think you've got the wrong chap.'

My partner floated down and stood next to me. She rubbed her chin and bit her lip in thoughtful repose, as she looked at me shivering. Taking gentle hold of my frozen hands, warmth surged inside, like liquid gold.

'Hmmm, not as easy as the last guy, but no worries, we'll get through, even if I have to—'

She didn't get to finish that sentence as the first massive rumble behind shook the ground beneath our feet.

'Oh shit, he's made it through. Thought we might have had a little longer. Dennis, we can discuss the ins and outs of why, what, and where later, but for now we need to go.' As she released her grip, the cold instantly crept back in.

I didn't feel the need to challenge her understanding of who I was, but looked forward, *if* the Reaper guy would permit, to finding out why I was here instead of this Dennis chap she kept on about.

She seemed annoyed that we had to leave so soon, hastily looking for an escape route whilst muttering angrily under her breath. Without any clue as to what was happening, I watched her whirl and swirl and wondered, what could possibly be worse than being nearly dead? Oh yeah, *really* dead.

Then suddenly she stopped and looked at me, the way you do when you've a stupid idea to share with the class.

'I need you to take a leap of faith. Hold my hand and *think* flying, not in a plane but on your own. Bit like Superman. Got that?'

'And then?'

Over the ridge, an enormous wall of snow raced our way, swollen and angry like a bad case of acne. No TV or doorway to jump into here. I looked up at the oncoming white express train and then to the woman.

She held my hand firmly.

'No time to be dull now, Dennis! Show me your true colours. You can do it, believe me.'

I closed my eyes tight and, in my idiocy, wished for forgiveness, rather than to fly.

And then I felt the air whistle past and hoped I'd taken to the air. But no. And then again yes, sort of. For my feet had left the ground, but I was tumbling and spinning uncontrollably just a few inches above it, as the mountain of ice bore down on us.

I wailed in agony at being such a twat. 'I can't get up!'

'Superman, Dennis, Superman, not Super bloody Mario! Get up here.'

Reaper's ice-cold fingers wrapped around my cartwheeling body as ear-splitting thunder banged and crashed. I don't know why the snow never buried me, but I expected to be a made-to-measure icicle for sure. And yet this wasn't to be my fate, for when I scraped the ice from my face, I was somehow soaring high above snow-covered peaks, green valleys, and beneath blue skies.

In shock, I looked nervously across for support, any support, only to be met with howls of laughter from my companion.

I bit my lip.

Our angry ice demon fell behind and was thankfully gone as we climbed higher and higher. With outstretched arms, I was soaring, flying, just as I remembered in my childhood dreams, long ago. So now I was doing just that; ducking, diving, wheeling, and turning. What was happening to me? How was this possible? It could only be a dream, couldn't it?

And when things seem too good to be true, they often are. In my crazy new world, why oh why would I ever *doubt* I was flying.

Reality came like a kick in the nuts, as I looked wide-eyed at the razor-sharp peaks below.

'Oh my god!'

My legs toggled between riding a bike and doing a breaststroke kick, whilst my arms doggy paddled. I was in serious trouble, miles up in nothingness without a parachute, and the granite teeth below were coming up bloody fast.

'Silly man, you don't know how to use a parachute,' my companion yelled.

'Help,' was all my lungs could manage.

'You nincompoop. Open your eyes. Now keep them open and for goodness' sake stop flapping. Just relax and let it all hang loose. Like you did when you were a kid. Like this!'

I flicked a quick glance in my freefalling panic, and there she was, lying on her back, gliding without a care in the world.

However, my mind was everywhere it shouldn't have been, as streaming eyes toggled between certain death and her perfect backstroke. Only then did I realise chilling – or was it swimming? –

was the only option I had.

As my lungs prepared to wail like a banshee, the upcoming rocky terrain stopped in its tracks. Shaking, both in fear and cold, I turned around nervously, only to see my companion grinning. She was clearly pleased, and for a change so was I.

As she beckoned me to join her high above, I wasn't going to disappoint. That would be rude.

You know, on reflection, during that terrifying fall, I thought I might see my life flash before me. But then again, that was nonsensical, as I hadn't yet had one, had I? The air was crystal clear; no sounds, no jets, no cars below, nothing but me soaring upward and onward. My flying skills, I'll admit, were a little rusty, but I'd long missed those forgotten dreams of clouds, rainbows, and spit spots of rain. I was thrilled to be back.

Until, that was, being wiped out by a flock of gulls. Fragments of bratwurst, fries, feathers and ice cream clouded the air, and once more I was out of control.

'Here, let me help.'

The woman flew to my side, gently holding my shaking arm and steadying me as we floated over miles of beautiful valleys, steep waterfalls, gorgeous alpine villages with warm sunshine flooding across blue snow below.

Eventually we drifted down toward an old alpine barn, nestling on the edge of fertile green pastures, with the melodious sounds of cow bells ringing in our arrival.

Two things, no, three things I thought of as we came in for a soft landing.

One: did I still have a vast hole in my trousers? For it had been a touch chilly in that neighbourhood as we'd soared high above.

Two: had I shat myself? For it sure felt odd down there.

And three: did she really know what I was thinking?

Walking on a few steps ahead, I watched her shoulders move up and down. Was she laughing? Ha! Of course she bloody was. She knew exactly what I was thinking.

But you know what worried me more?

Who was Reaper?

5. Thingamajig

As we walked the uneven pathway, past sun-kissed meadows, the healing rays began melting much of the darkness I'd felt on this hellish journey. As butterflies and insects flew up from the verge, my mind meandered like a stream. Even Reaper fell off my radar.

And then I just stopped, there on that track, wanting no more than *that* moment to last forever. But just as the sound of my companion's footsteps faded, so fear nudged me in the ribs. Even amongst such beauty, there were things I desperately needed to know, and without a moment to lose, I ran to join my companion.

I skidded to a dusty halt as she turned and paused for me to catch my breath. But before she could say anything, I blurted, 'I've got a few—'

'Questions. Yes, I know. 1,000,002, to be precise.'

'I'm sorry, are you kidding me?'

'Well, that's one less; only 1,000,001 now.'

'How can I possibly have that many questions? That's ridiculous.'

'So you think. What's the most important question right now?'

The answer seemed both obvious and relevant. 'What the bloody hell is going on?'

'Good question; to be repeated 177,422 times. It's certainly one of your biggest questions and takes a hefty chunk out of the total.'

My jaw dropped open long enough for the local insect population to roost in there. She was making no sense whatsoever. Although she seemed satisfied with her reply, I was not.

'So, you know how many times I'm going to ask you a question?'

'Yeah.'

'I don't think so.'

'Your choice, but what is, is!'

'So, if I have over a million questions and I ask one per second, without eating, drinking, peeing, going to work and sleeping, how long would that—'

'Take? Eleven-point-five days, give or take ten seconds.'

She looked at me with her arms folded, ready to take my next foolish question. I quite expected her to answer before I'd even asked it. Luckily she let me ask it anyway.

'Where are we?'

It seemed a very good question to me.

I think she was being flippant when she said, 'Take a look around, Dennis.'

But so compelling was her direction, I did just that, and once again meandering became a thing. She snapped me back with, 'So, do you want to know *where* we are or how many times you'll ask me that?'

Miss Bossy Boots put me on edge. 'Both.'

'I know I've answered as many questions as we've had time for but try not to ask multiple questions. They take up far too much time and, as per the Department of F and D guidelines, I'm only obliged to answer the last one.'

You could have knocked me down with a lead feather. The Department of F&D. What the bloody hell's that?

'Fate and Destiny.'

With lips tightly pursed, I shook my head slowly. But I could see she wasn't impressed either, knowing I had over a million questions to ask during the time we'd supposedly spend together.

Disapproval crossed her face.

'Just because you have a million or so questions, doesn't mean

I have answers for all of them, or answers you want to hear. But to keep you from getting over stressed on details, let me start with your second question: 15,273. And the first one, I don't know?'

That took me by surprise.

'Brilliant! So you're a mathematical clever clogs who's lost.'

We walked slowly onward, this time side by side.

'Where's your compass, young lady?'

'Travelling through new dimensions, time and space is much more flexible, so doesn't require magnets and twirly needles. Everywhere, for your information, leads us to where we need to go, something like a Sat Nav. Sometimes we get roadworks up here too, and diversions without diversion signs. It's easy to get muddled and so damn annoying, especially when you're in a hurry.'

'Intergalactic detour? I think I've heard everything now.'

'I doubt that.'

It all sounded very peculiar or was it just me? I wasn't convinced.

'And where might we be going then, you and I?'

'Home!'

'Really?'

'No, of course not. Getting caught is not an option and your home isn't safe right now. He'd be waiting. But I have an idea. Well, sort of a plan, a thingamajig.'

'Thingamajig, hey? Hmmm, how about food, new trousers, or a fast car perhaps?'

'Huh, you make me laugh!'

I wished the feeling was mutual.

We kept on walking until we reached the outskirts of the village and crept into an old, rickety barn, full of soft hay, a few farm items and, luckily, little else.

'Think we'll stop here the night. What say you, Robin of Sherwood?'

'Who? Someone else in here?'

'No, I was being light-hearted. Couldn't you tell?'

'You mocketh me. For too long hath thou been in the theatre, my fair lady?'

I couldn't believe I just said that.

My companion bowed low and slow.

'Well saideth, Wobin.'

We dropped down into the hay and laughed like school kids. This was ludicrous and worrying all rolled into one.

'When was the last time you laughed, Dennis?'

That was a random question, and if I was honest, I couldn't really remember. 'I dunno.'

'Twenty-three years ago, on your fourth birthday,' she nonchalantly chirped. 'If we ever get the chance, we should work on that laugh of yours.'

That didn't make the point any less random, or me happier – but how did she know? Whether her point was valid under the circumstances I didn't know, but I was no less worried and confused than when this nightmare journey began.

'Okay, here's the bottom line,' she said, 'and I make no apologies for this. At some point, as you know, Death will come for you, for you are mortal and that comes at a price. You won't be aware when Death loiters nearby, but near-misses on the road, too much alcohol, banging your head, or failing to have regular check-ups with the doctor are moments when he lingers longer, just in case. *He's* never far away.'

She was serious, so I kept quiet and continued to follow her line of thought. It wasn't easy.

'Keep with me here, Dennis. Sometimes mistakes are made and that's a part of human nature, isn't it? Yet it's also the nature of everything, and an annoying feature within realms and other dimensions you can't see or understand. Nowhere is perfect.'

At that point, she raised her eyes to the ceiling and held her gaze on the wooden beams above.

My eyes followed. 'Mmmmm,' was all I could manage, as if I understood. I don't think she was convinced I was following. I certainly knew dull was as far away from perfect as you could get. Perhaps I was a mistake, perhaps this all was. And yet dull and dreary seemed to sum up completely the fug that was me.

'Fug, hey, that's interesting, because I get that too.' She frowned again, like she'd remembered something, and bit her lip as though it was important. 'What family do you have?'

It was another surprising question in amongst the chaos. 'None, that I know of. You know, that's weird, isn't it?'

'Can't think of anyone in your past? Parents, perhaps?'

I thought hard. Unhappily, the fug of nothingness was all I could remember.

She stepped in. 'I know you're having a difficult time right now, but what I say next might shine a light on some of this.'

'Really?'

'Hope so. You might want to sit.'

So, in two minutes and twenty-seven seconds precisely, she outlined a long-buried tragedy, where only one occupant in a crash on the village outskirts of Little Glum survived. The Angel of Death swooped, ready to claim his third soul of the day, but unexpectedly a young midwife came by and pulled that body from the mangled wreckage. Death and his understudy, the Grim Reaper, missed their chance to claim the life of that little four-year-old boy.

Trauma, as I now discovered, seemed to have been with me ever since.

The gift of life wasn't Death's mercy. No, that belonged to the midwife. But Death's lieutenant wouldn't forget losing his quota and marked me for putting off till tomorrow what he desperately wanted to do that day.

So there it was. The day of judgement had finally caught up with me. Yet like a crashing wave, I knew I wasn't ready. Why would I be? My partner skipped over my upbringing, saying questions would have to wait for another time.

I felt drained to exhaustion. How many times can I nearly die?

'Dennis, it's not luck you're alive, its more complicated than that. Sometimes, in your absent-minded, dullest moments, you've taken unnecessary risks and been a gnat's tit away from dying. Yet here you are. Even Death makes mistakes, and in your case, one's been made. Not for the first time. As I tried to say before, that's why I'm here.'

Despite her attempt to cheer me, how was I supposed to deal with such a sad summary of life's bullet points? However, I now realised my tedious existence and the fug surrounding my past resulted not from nature, but somehow from spite. I tried absorbing the significance of it all, but she jumped in, failing to read the room.

'Any questions? Oh yeah, I'd forgotten, you've got a mountain of questions, haven't you?'

Before I could say 'not now', she followed up with something more encouraging. 'Okay! Ask me three questions and then we'll have something to eat. After that I'll sort out your trousers as a freebie. Saves you asking.'

So there I was, looking at my backside, trying to make sense of what she'd said. To recap...

'I can hear you, you know.'

'Just get out of my head for a minute then, will you?'

'Okay.'

There was silence, no white noise, nothing. I felt clothed again.

'What waist size are you?' she called over.

I growled.

'Never mind. I know anyhow, just messing with you. I'll keep out of your head, I promise. Get recapping.'

As I was saying, or was I thinking? I don't know, I'm confused.

Anyway, I'm not dead but should be. I've been kidnapped by someone I don't yet know but to whom I feel a little gratitude. We're running away from something very bad that's specifically after me. I've flown, which was cool, torn my trousers, worryingly leapt through a TV and a wee small door and was almost buried under an avalanche. And yet through all that, I haven't died or shat myself. And to top it all, I now know why I tick the dull way I do. I only hope there's chance before the end for my tick to turn into a tock.

I turned to my partner.

She looked at me and got herself comfortable. 'I'm ready.'

'There are far too many questions, but here goes. Number one: what's coming for me?'

'That's simple enough. The Grim Reaper! Next.'

I truly couldn't stop myself. 'Fuck me!'

She gave me such a filthy look. 'Huh, only if he catches you, and I'm not planning for that this shift. I think that was more of an option than a question, don't you? Carry on.'

'That worries me more than you can possibly understand. Okay, number two: who are you?'

'Ahhh, can we skip that one and go to number three?'

'Why?'

'Because I know you're hungry and eating will take less time than answering number two. Dennis, just say yes. Pleeeease?'

I could sense anguish from my normally composed companion, so I chose the most immediate need and plumped for an easy win.

'Okay, number three: what's for tea?'

No sooner had I thought about what I fancied than hot fish and chips and condiments appeared. She was good!

Without ceremony, I dug in. 'You not having any? Its fantast—'

'Not while I'm at work. Can't fly if I get too heavy; I won't take off, I'll just bounce. No, I'll just watch you.'

She seemed to be smiling but I reckoned it was a grimace.

'No, I'm smiling. Honest.'

Her grin widened further.

But as food avalanched down my front, my companion's gaze was putting me off. She needed to concentrate on something else, not my eating habits.

'You could answer number two whilst I'm eating.'

As she began, the demands of the day had a way of catching up. I'd never felt so exhausted. I nodded when I shouldn't and yawned far too much as she mapped out the intricacies of our existence whilst keeping an eye on me and any hidden dangers.

And then, as she got to the part I really wanted to know, the sixty-five-hour day got the better of me. The instant I'd taken my last mouthful, my eyelids dopped like a well-oiled drawbridge.

But in the moment, just before my lids slammed tight, I managed to mutter one last question.

'Who *are* you?'

I didn't hear her reply.

The sleep had no dreams. It was jet black. No chases. No Grim Reaper, nothing. I guess it was just the rest my frazzled body needed.

Yet I could have been just plain dead.

I wouldn't have known.

6. ☹◆■♋[1]

It felt like a warm morning but smelled like February. Jet lag perhaps, or COVID? Anyway, I felt refreshed, but we were not in the barn. Here I was on a lounger, beside an infinity pool, overlooking a lovely blue sea, distant hills and far away mountains. The scene was like nothing I'd ever seen, and it simply took my breath away. Birds spun and reeled high above, and I could hear the faint rumble of distant traffic. Much better that than the thunderous sounds of *you know who*. Strange that I didn't remember how we got here.

'Hi there, sleepyhead. Wow, don't you snore!'

I smacked my dry lips, rubbed the crispy bits from my eyes, and stretched. 'And I love you too. What a cracking way to greet the living dead in the morning.'

My abductor was sitting on the edge of another lounger, busying herself with papers on her lap. Untidy piles of notes and diagrams surrounded her perfect feet. This was the first time I'd had chance to look at her closely. I didn't actually know what or who she was. Maybe she was an angel and maybe this was a bad dream, that just wouldn't bugger off.

She looked up.

'Hey, can I ask—'

'I'm Luna,' she shouted over.

'Oh, okay, caught me there, didn't you? Is that it, just Luna? I thought it might be a little more like Helga or Miss Trunchbull perhaps.'

---

1 Luna

'Very funny, I'm sure. Well, Mr Sarcastic, my technical name is much longer, which you won't remember or be able to pronounce.'

'No, go on, I'm sorry, please tell me your name. I'm pretty good with names.'

'Do you remember Supercalifragilisticexpialidocious?'

'Huh, doesn't everyone on the planet?'

'This planet, yes. Well, it's a bit like that, a bit of a mouthful.'

'Go on. You know who I am.'

'Okay if you insist, but I did warn you. It's ☜●●✻ ♌♏⚷✻ ◆♏●●✻◆♏♍ ⚷⬚●✻ ◼♌⚏● ☐◼♌⚏ ○☐☐◼[2]

'Bloody hell, that is a mouthful. Luna it is then.'

She smiled warmly and stuck her tongue out.

'Sorry about yesterday and all the commotion. You've a right to be annoyed, but I've thick skin and I'm used to it these days. Anyhow, you fell asleep before I'd finished, and yes, I guess I have abducted you, for the right reason. But you'll be pleased to know I won't be conducting experiments on you, not like those off-world alien types. Gahhh, they're creepy.'

Experiments? Aliens?

Those thoughts hadn't crossed my mind and yet now the idea of sexual deviancy was difficult to forget.

'So, who are you really? Not an alien, I guess.' Then my mouth took me somewhere my brain didn't want to go. 'Er, not that sexual deviancy with you would be bad. Oh heck, no, I mean you and I having…Erm, no, sorry I'll shut up, shall I?'

Luna was frowning, nodding and looking a little red.

'That's one hell of a hole you've dug, Dennis. Deviancy isn't on the menu, as far as I know.'

I stopped, for I knew we were well off topic and for the sake of further embarrassment needed to get back to establishing who she was.

'I don't remember you telling me what you are?'

2 Ellibekiwelliweckylingalongamoon

'Yeah, I did. You were out of it before I noticed you'd actually dropped off. Didn't want to wake you unless Reaper turned up. And lo and behold he did, so I thought it best to leave quickly. You were sound asleep, so I carried you in my pocket for a few weeks before I was able to give him the slip.' Luna gazed wistfully into the distance. 'Nice place this, isn't it? Thought you'd like somewhere less stressful.'

'How close did he get?'

'About as far from me as you are.'

'Bloody hell!'

And then I noticed a stained bandage around her wrist. Luna shuffled uneasily. I guessed taking me wasn't a picnic in the park.

'We flew around for a few weeks? Not hours, but weeks? You are joking, right?'

'To be honest, it was a shade longer.'

She was hiding something. I just knew it.

'All this fresh air; it's just what we need.'

'Luna. Just how long have I been asleep?'

She winced. 'Three and a half—'

'Weeks? I've been asleep three and a half weeks? Christ.'

Her face didn't change. The wince remained. There was more.

'No. Longer? Months?'

'If you count loo stops and the odd passing conversation, in disguise of course, then yes it was about three and a half…Such a lovely place, isn't it?'

She was off again and walked a few steps across to the shimmering pool.

'Oh no you don't. Three and a half…?'

The game was up, and I wanted my pound of flesh.

Luna dipped her toe gently into the water and wiggled it slowly.

'Right, yes, okay, it was longer than I'd expected, but three and a half years is nothing when you're out of it and I'm doing all the hard work. No meaningful conversations or even chit chat. Oh, and I had to take you to the toilet and feed you. It's not all fun and games and—'

'STOP! Just stop!'

My head felt like a pressure cooker, about to pop clean off my shoulders. I stood motionless for a good half hour before she returned with a cup of tea. I was many things: dazed, confused, stunned, astounded, and couldn't move a muscle. That's three and a half birthdays I'd missed.

Luna waved her hand in front of my eyes to gauge the depth of shock.

I didn't blink, I couldn't.

'Hmmm, you're taking it better than I thought you would,' she said casually, and walked off sipping her hot tea.

I remained frozen to the spot, assimilating the hopelessness of my predicament.

'Oh, if you find crumbs in your hair, that's me, sorry, but I needed a biscuit or two to keep me going. Would have preferred something a little healthier, but beggars can't be choosers when they're on the run.'

I felt very insignificant if I was being totally honest. And at that, I shook my head, snapping out of my comatose hell. Before I had the sense to say anything worthwhile, my hands went to my head, frantically rubbing my greasy locks. How do you hope to exorcise three and a half years of pocket fluff, without crucifix-shaped fingers?

Sure enough, pieces of ginger nut fell to the ground, almost enough for a meal. Yet, in the rubbing of my scalp, the smell of sweets wafted out. It wasn't Liquorice Allsorts that was for sure.

'What else have I been sleeping with for all that bloody time?'

Luna left the ripples radiating across the pool and stepped over.

'Oh, I might have had a few chews in there, and Parma Violets. Ohhh, there were a few coins, hair grips, tissues, that sort of thing.

But *these* are my favourites.' With a warm smile she held open a pack of Love Hearts. 'Go on, take one.'

My instinct was to shout and scream about the loss of three and a half years of my life, or three and a half dull birthdays, but do you know what? I couldn't be arsed. Everything so far had been madness, so why not a few years! And yet I hesitated, thinking about my lifeless body flopping around in her pockets, mixing with all that junk. Eurgh! But then again, I was safe, wasn't I?

With a degree of gratitude, I accepted the sweet of long forgotten memories. First, I had to pick off a few stubborn pieces of fluff.

'Luna, next time, wake me up.'

She nodded.

I turned the little sweet over, curious to see what it said inside the heart.

'I haven't had one of these in years.'

ROCKET MAN

That sounded a little more exciting than the usual dull offerings like ALWAYS or BE HAPPY. It tasted good, too.

'Quick question. Did you clean my teeth when I was…?'

Luna tutted loudly. 'Nope, just popped an Allsort in; your favourite.'

She was dead right there. I looked on eagerly as she pulled hers from the packet. A yellow one, without fluff.

'What does it say?'

Luna blushed. 'Not saying!'

'But you must!'

'Why?'

'It's playground law, you know that. C'mon, show me.'

Luna slowly held out her hand. The sweet was face down. 'Dennis Foster, it's *just* a sweet, not a fortune cookie.'

'But I told you mine. What's the problem?'

'If it's that important, turn it over.'

Hoping to make fun out of her absurd message, I turned it over. But as I did so, I sensed a certain awkwardness. For on the sweet was the heart and inside that heart was L&D.

She snatched back the sweet.

'Happy now!' she snapped, then popped it into her mouth.

'What does L and D mean? Er, Lost and Dull? I'm not certain I know that one.'

'Dennis, it's *not* too difficult. Use your head; but it's not dull.'

I searched the recesses of my mind, which didn't take long, and tried some combinations. Lick & Dust? Like & Don't? Light & Dark? No that wasn't it.

Luna watched the cogs turn slowly in the mush I called a brain and shook her head in disbelief.

'Hmmm, what about Luna and Den…?'

By the time the penny dropped, Luna had disappeared. This whole business was getting crazier by the minute, and I was lost for words. Now I had a dozen more questions to add to my list. But these weren't about me for a change, they were about her, and me and her.

Confused? Yep, join the club.

When I found her, she'd settled on an outcrop of rock overlooking a stunning valley and distant lake, which flickered like foil in the sunshine. Multi-coloured flowers were in abundance and a heady fragrance passed softly over this quiet stoney outcrop. Luna sat framed in the moment, scribbling notes, umming and ahhing over stuff. I wasn't certain that this was the time to disturb her, but it was abundantly clear she wasn't altogether happy.

'Was it something I said? Was it about the sweet?'

Luna looked up and glared at me with pursed lips. I knew something was going on inside that pretty head of hers, but nothing was coming out. She looked away and continued to scribble. It was the first time I'd had chance to look at her. I mean, really look.

As far as my pea brain could tell, she was older than me, maybe mid to late thirties? But it was hard to tell as her features shimmered and shifted. Her face was a darker shade of pale, lightly peppered with freckles. Two silver rings pierced the side of her nose, but across her brow and neck, she carried a number of deep scars. Remarkably, I hadn't noticed them and guessed these were stories I'd rather not know about, or she'd rather not tell.

She was my sort of height, with blue eyes. She was slim, unlike me; she was polite, a bit like me; and attractive. Definitely not like me. Her dark hair hung down her back in delightful double braided locks and mingling in those strands, a long glowing silver streak.

She reminded me of someone, but for the life of me I couldn't place her. What I did know was she was smart, unlike me…brave, unlike me, and I wouldn't want to get on her wrong side. Ever!

Her clothes changed every time we got to somewhere new. I guess she had an extensive collection for all types of adventures in far-flung places. But today she wore a lightweight blouse, light coloured trousers and was barefoot. Sunglasses balanced on top of her head, finishing off the casual look. She was not the type I'd ever expect to bump into on the streets back home, yet here we were, my partner and I, peas in a coffin-shaped pod. Who'd have guessed.

Then I remembered the train crash state of my trousers. I spun around and looked down.

'They're new, don't worry. Your butt's well-hidden and clean. I made certain of that!'

I sneered. 'You did what?'

'Nothing a wash down with a good old fashioned hose pipe couldn't sort out. You're clean and tidy, so stop worrying. Now you're ready for almost anything, Dennis.'

'Right, on that note, before anything else. I'm not Dennis Foster. Why do you keep calling me that?'

'Because that's you!'

'Not the last time I looked. I'm…er…erm…Jason Bourne?'

'Oh no you're not. You're Dennis Foster!'

'Arnold Schwarzenegger?'

'Nope.'

'King Charles the third?'

'Good try, but you are who you are.'

'You've got the wrong person, I'm…ggg…rr…lll…I'm… ggdhg…ror…lell…'

I couldn't remember. I couldn't remember my own bloody name. Letters tumbled out with no sense, no rhyme, nor reason, just gobbledegook. Sounded like I was demented. However hard I tried, I couldn't spit it out. Only spit.

'What's happened to me? What have you done?'

'Nothing. Calm down. You are Dennis Foster. My file on you is sound, and I'm never wrong. Well, that's not exactly true. I made a mistake in the fifteenth century which didn't go down too well, but other than that, you are who you are. Anyway, it's on your birth certificate.' She waved an official looking document in the air. 'Maybe you've just forgotten, or wanted to forget?'

'What does that mean?' I pranced around like a Tellytubby trying to grab the piece of paper.

It was hopeless. She was much too quick and body swerved my efforts like a prima ballerina. I stopped, feeling down in the mouth, looking the glum bum I was.

'Luna, what am I mixed up in? I really don't understand. As I look around, everything seems real enough but there's so many things going on at once. Flapping that piece of paper about is not helping.'

I retraced my steps back to the lounger and sank down, growling loudly. Dropping her scribbled notes here and there, Luna did her best to keep up, but rather than being defiant as I half expected, she sat down heavily on her lounger and dropped her head into her hands. She began to weep.

I looked over, sighed heavily and growled again. If anyone should be sobbing, I surmised, it should be me. But as exasperated as I was, being chased by death and being called Dennis, the only concern I had right now was for this crazy lady.

The sound of her sniffles hit deep down. As I stood over Luna's hunched shoulders, I couldn't fail to notice the mountain of yellow Post-it notes upon which copious scribbles and crossings out littered their surface. I gently touched her shoulder as tears plip plopped through her fingers and dripped onto the notes.

'Luna, why are you upset?' It was a simple question and well meant.

In amongst the sniffs, tears and between her wet fingers, she burbled, 'I'm hopeless.'

Her wailing threw me a bit. Tough though she seemed on the outside, perhaps inside other things were going on? *Women's* things? I dismissed that notion promptly; it wasn't an avenue of expertise and, well, let's just leave it there.

So, getting back to Luna, I felt it time for a little support, you know, one-on-one.

'With my most sincere and utmost thanks,' I started cheerily, 'it was *you* who saved me from certain death. How can that *not* be good? You're not hopeless, you're...'

'Lost.'

'Wasn't exactly what I had in mind, but...excuse me? We're what?'

Luna didn't repeat her last, but slowly lifted her head from her wet hands, and through flushed wet cheeks, smiled a look of surprise. 'No one's ever thanked me before.'

'Look, despite losing three and a half birthdays, I, for one, am very grateful that you abducted me. Who couldn't be? Everyone should be abducted at least once in their dull lives to—'

'Dennis, I get it.' She sniffed. 'You can stop now.'

She wiped her nose on her sleeve and looked down to the Post-its, desperately trying to make sense of her notes. Doubt was etched across her face.

I thought saving my arse might be straightforward, but clearly it wasn't. I was worried about my dejected companion, and it seemed to me she was putting a full load of red pants in a white wash. I thought it best to keep quiet about the pants.

However complicated it was, Luna needed to slow down and follow through with one issue at a time. Easy for dull old me to say, but she was struggling; even I could see that. So I sat down beside her and took her wet hand in mine and squeezed it gently.

'Just because you don't ask for help in this mad place, doesn't mean you shouldn't. I'm not actually certain what I can do for you, but I'd be happy if you asked anyway.'

Luna looked up and hope flickered for a moment.

'Whatever you can do for me, I'll be forever grateful, even if your mate Reaper gets me.'

'He's *not* my mate.'

'Well, maybe, but I'm actually okay with that. Of course, I'd rather it was a lot later, say in sixty years, I won't lie. But I'm not certain where I go from here, wherever here actually is. I'm the one who's lost on so many levels and as far as I'm concerned, only you can *help*.'

Providing opportunity for Lady Luck to also lend a hand, I crossed my fingers tightly, out of sight.

'I can still hear you.'
Damn.

7. Guardian Good Luck

As the day wore on, Luna seemed to settle down a little as she pored over and over her scribbles. I couldn't make head nor tails of the stuff, whichever way I turned the note. However, I must admit it felt good not being as useless as I thought I was, though I sensed Luna was pulling something from inside, deep inside; something I'd long forgotten or, in fact, never used.

Empathy.

'May I sit with you, Luna?'

She looked up blank faced, and I suspect she thought I'd sit somewhere other than her lounger.

Unfortunately, but not unexpectedly, gravity, inertia and other science stuff, foresaw the collision.

As I sat down, the lounger snapped in the middle, throwing us together with the force of a medieval catapult. My nose embedded itself into her forehead as her dart-like pen impaled my trainer.

No harm, no foul, but it was classic farce.

As our sandwiched bodies fell clumsily out of the metal framework onto the dusty ground, I coughed, and she spluttered. I don't think she saw the funny side, but Chaplin would've.

I tried again.

'I might be dull as dishwater, Luna, but despite what just happened, I have every confidence in you.' I pulled her battered pen from my foot and sheepishly offered it back, happily declaring, 'So, where to next, partner?'

Luna burst into tears…again.

I slumped, hoping the tears would end soon. But no. Yet as I sat without ideas or absorbent handkerchief, a flaming cocktail appeared unannounced in my hand, together with parasols and olives. It swirled bright green and smelled rather wonderful.

Watching out for the flames and my nose, I took a quick sip.

WOW!

'Luna. Try this!'

'What is it?' She sniffed and looked up.

'It's a drink, what do you think it is? It's like napalm but without the aftertaste. It's fantastic. This will certainly put hairs on your ches…Oh never mind. You're gonna love it.'

'But I don't drink. I can drink, but you know drinking and flying can be very dangerous. That's how Reaper gets a lot of his work.'

I wasn't going to take no for an answer and pushed the drink beneath her nose, making certain her face and hair didn't get singed. 'There's no alcohol in this. Trust me, I'm a barman!'

Though she was clearly feeling out of sorts, Luna decided to take a leap of faith, and sipped.

'Wow!'

One sip quickly became a gulp and within an instant, the drink and flames had gone.

I'd hoped to have another sip before it disappeared, but as that thought lingered, another drink appeared in my hand.

'You doing this?'

'Nope, it's all you, Dennis. Thank you.'

'For what? Showing a lady a good time?'

I laughed nervously.

'Huh, lady. That's very sweet of you. But not everything's as it seems; you should know that by now.'

'You're not a lady?'

'Not quite.'

'A guy?'

'Idiot!' Luna threw back the burning napalm and another and another before I could stop her. 'I don't just fly around all day rescuing cats from ♦□ℳℳ♦[3] you know. I'm highly trained in martial ◌□♦❖, ●◌■℈♦◌℈ℳ♦,[4] weapons, ℳ⊠□●□♦⊁❖ℳ♦[5] and cookery. There's nothing deadlier that my Vindaloo.'

Luna giggled and then laughed out loud, frightening off the birds who'd gathered to watch the entertainment.

To hear her relaxed and a bit tiddly was as delightful as it was worrying.

'I have no idea what you've just said, so let's *not* have another drink. Let's just calm down and have a strong coffee instead. Don't you think?'

She was none too keen on sobering up and it took me ages to grab new drinks off her as they miraculously appeared in her hands. Naivety on my part was clearly to blame for the resultant scrappy punch up, and I'm pleased to say no human was hurt in the making of the mess.

The once-perfect setting beside the pool now resembled the carnage of a Roman lion pit. Eventually brawn overcame brain, or so I felt, but it didn't feel right sitting on top of my saviour. Yet it was the only way I could get coffee into her system.

After she'd stopped squirming beneath me, she agreed to take her hot black medicine.

She spluttered. 'Ergh.'

'Go on, don't be a baby, have another sip. It'll clear your head, eventually. Then we need to plan our escape to somewhere far away from that certified nightmare.'

Without warning, Luna slumped beneath me and something cracked.

Christ! I leapt up, thinking I'd broken her. I had, her mood.

'♄☡, ↗♦ℳ&;□↗↗!'[6]

She wasn't happy, that was for sure, so I stepped carefully back, erring on the side of caution. Luna pulled herself to her feet, leaving

---

3 trees
4 arts, languages
5 explosives
6 Oh, fuck off

three broken cocktail glasses on the ground where I'd pinned her. At least she wasn't crying.

We recovered our composure, tidying up the battleground beside the pool, giggling over our wild antics.

Forgive the pun, but it was a tonic for sure, and it was exactly what Luna needed to get her shit together. We went over options, which were sadly in short supply. But, as we chatted through the issues, I discovered more about my newfound friend than I think she'd willingly have offered, without a drop of hooch to loosen her tongue.

'How old did you say you were, Luna?'

As we talked, she accepted she was overwhelmed by her own disorganisation. This was a default position, as was the anxiety that flowed through her when things weren't going well.

I thought this whole crazy business must be normal and my abduction was right on track, give or take a bump or two. But I was wrong.

She was determined to save me and my soul, absolutely, except things weren't going strictly to her chaotic plan. In fact, she was flying by the seat of her pants, almost out of control. Who could tell?

'So your plan has a few holes in it. I've never made—'

'Dennis,' Miss Anxiety interrupted, 'it *shouldn't* have holes. When it does, I'm not doing my job right. The more it goes off course, the more overwhelmed I get. It's a nightmare!'

And hence the waterworks. I got it. The more she revealed the more I realised she had more demons inside her than were following me. Even with all that internal chaos, I still had faith in her, blind maybe, but in her defence I wasn't completely dead yet, was I?

For all my own failings, she was anything but useless and certainly not boring like me. She was beguiling and charming and as helpful a person, or thingy, as I'd ever found, to the point I had to ask, 'If your mate Reaper is Death personified, does his day job really well, except for the odd mistake, then where does that put you in the great scheme of it all? I know your name, but what are you?'

'You've asked that before, but I didn't get chance to tell you. Not wanting to sound weird, I'm an angel, your guardian, from the Department of Fate and Destiny. If I get you home safe—'

'You mean *when* you get me home!'

'Yes, of course. When you're back home safe, I'll head off to a new posting.' She looked wistfully out into wild, black nothingness. 'Somewhere out there in a distant galaxy maybe.'

'I'm not certain I understand, but an angel? My guardian angel? Wow. With all those powers, how hard can this job—'

'How hard? How bloody hard! It's not easy trying to guide you when you don't listen or do listen then do something completely different. You don't get the blame, we do. It can be very challenging, this eternal life of ours. So let me ask you, Dennis, how often have you asked for help in your life?'

'All the time. I'm forever aski—'

'I *know*! I've been listening to you for years and guiding you time and time again. But you never seem to listen. I *can* shout when I have to, you know, but I'm sorry to say I never seem to be able to get through to you. I've screamed my head off, but you've never once listened. It's said that ⬠□◆ ♏⌾■ ◆⌾&♏ ⌾ ⌆□□•♏ ◆□ •⌾◆♏□, ♌◆◆ ⬠□◆ ♏⌾■'◆ ⍥⌾&♏ ⍊⋈⭘ ♌□⋈■&.'[7]

'Luna, I can't understand what you're saying. I need subtitles or footnotes or something.'

'Oh, sorry. I said, you can take a horse to water, but you can't make him drink! That's been you.'

I felt an idiot. Here I was, beyond dull, understanding what she meant. It was true, I had this one-way relationship with those above,

---

7 you can take a horse to water, but you can't make him drink

asking for this and that, but never actually realising my problems could have been prevented. I always looked at the glass half empty when in fact I was being told time and time again that it was at least half full.

How could I not forget pummelling the computer in the office. All I'd had to do was leave, for god's sake, whilst poor Luna was trying her best to direct me. Look what happens when you don't listen!

In that moment a torrent of older memories and lost chances rattled like a train through my pea brain. A tremendous sneeze hit those thoughts like a full stop.

Luna jumped in surprise. 'Do you know what sneezes are?'

I glanced around the nearby fields and took a deep breath. 'Hay fever?'

'Maybe, but they're also your acceptance of my guidance. Now there's a thing that's taken longer than I'd hoped. Bless you.'

I looked at her and knew she could see right through me, for the fool I'd been. I felt incredibly lonely and vulnerable, with a mind stuck in some distant void.

She broke into my silent world, gently.

'Dennis, I think we're beginning to understand each other. I don't know about you, but I think it's time for a change. How about another chance to get home and do the things you should've done?'

My eyes filled with tears.

Luna took me and my sniffles into her arms and squeezed softly.

'Listen, I try to be focused but it rarely works. I get side-tracked and then I over analyse. When I have a plan, a list of things that should be done, I get caught up in the minutiae of the moment. We all have our failings and I have more than most. It drives me to distraction, but it's not what we haven't got that's important. It's what we have that makes the difference. They are themselves superpowers if we acknowledge and understand them. However, we both know we all need a little push now and then.'

We sighed simultaneously, for it seemed that both of us were incomplete and this was not just my journey, but ours.

In a moment of frustration, she threw a handful of Post-its up high. Flitting and fluttering like butterflies, they headed off without care into the blue sky.

'Dennis, I spend too long in one place without getting the job done. I get all anxious and then feel guilty. It's a right mess. I'm a mess, I should say, that's why it's already taken me two attempts to rescue you. It took one hundred and seventy-six attempts to rescue the six before you. I'm hopeless, I know I am.'

I didn't have anything to say. The numbers seemed questionable, but looking to Luna in an angelic crisis seemed perfectly logical and therefore okay. We *all* make mistakes. And whilst my mouth felt like it might never close, my sorrowful partner was welling up. I had a tsunami of questions to ask, but this wasn't the time.

However, as I looked at Luna, I knew at last my glass was pretty much half full.

'Look, you have a mission, crucial for my survival. I need you to spin your magic and I know you can do it. We need a simple plan, which includes Plan B and C options, should *you know who* get in our way. And, by the look of the sky over there on the horizon, we might need to make haste. So, my friend, cheer up, all's not yet lost. Anyhow, third time lucky, hey? No pressure!'

I offered my hand. 'Are you ready?'

Luna didn't bother to shake my hand but stepped forward and gave me another hug. Calming herself, she drew in a deep breath, sniffed, and wiped her dripping nose on my sleeve.

I looked at the slimy trail. 'Oh, gross!'

'That's guardian good luck, Dennis,' she proudly declared.

Even in this strange playground of ours, I had my suspicions.

'Are you ready for a rough ride home, young man?'

'Oh yes!'

'Then it's time to paaaaarrrtay!'

I grabbed Luna's hand and looked upward. She did the same, and in those mad moments, I knew she was the best friend I'd ever have.

'Really?' she asked.

'Don't make a big deal of it.'

She beamed.

This was the Luna I needed, and with that, hand in hand, we soared like a rocket to the heavens above, seeking a place we hoped we'd be safe.

8. Pens, Pencils, Sharpener

We tore through Earth's upper atmospheres in the time it takes to make a good hot cuppa. Luna and I went over her plan to head to a place Reaper wouldn't go, agreeing on the basis of logic that Mars was definitely a place where no human footprint had been left, nor life lost. Thereby, Reaper had no purpose to go there, and as far as his pursuit was concerned, I put the threat cautiously on the backburner.

The ride, forgive the pun, was out of this world, as Luna and I bounced off whirling space debris and spun through moonbeams in an effort to leave the dark peril behind. As we raced through the inky darkness, my pale blue home became smaller and smaller, whilst the moon loomed large up ahead, grey and soulless.

As we fast approached the looming disc, it suddenly struck me; the notion that is, not the moon. What about air? Ah, but I was already in space, wasn't I, without a space suit, just my work hoody. Air, it seemed, was everywhere I needed it, thank god, and mercifully no gulls. However, as we travelled at warp speed, I noticed my feet and the bottoms of my legs, were turning blue.

'Is that supposed to happen?' I shouted across the void, pointing to my feet and now the tops of my legs.

'Don't worry, it's cosmetic. Just don't think about it.'

'Easy for you to say, you've not turned blue.'

But she was right. They looked awful, but I couldn't feel a thing as the ice crystals bloomed ever outward and upward. It looked like a bad case of fungus as crystals crept across my chest. Here was a man-sized gelato, hurtling through space. What a sight.

However, my attention moved from mere cosmetics to what was going on in my mouth.

My tongue probed, knowing something wasn't right. A side effect, maybe, of sucking in the void at stupid speed. Anyhow, my tongue pushed and poked and that's when I stopped hurtling and waited in the midst of nothingness. Something was happening, and I didn't like it; nope, not one bit. Discovering a wobbling tooth is unnerving at the best of times but, in the blink of an eye, tooth one fell out. There in front of my face, a little ivory object, soaked in spit and blood, hovered in the sunlight.

'Oh no.'

I grabbed the little bugger with an iced hand, whilst my tongue searched for more. And as God is my witness, more of the little sods started to wiggle. What was this, space sickness? It must be a lack of sleep, lack of food, lack of air, space scurvy or simply a lack of sense.

My mouth was swimming in teeth, but I wasn't about to spit them out. I needed them!

And then the weirdest thing loomed up in front. Coming up fast and a little too close for comfort was a gigantic asteroid.

It wasn't alone, for in its wake there were a hundred more, some bigger, some smaller. I swerved one way then the other to avoid collision. What were they and why did they look just like...?

Were they rocks? The shape wasn't what I thought asteroids would be. These were polished white with dark patches in amongst the curves.

Surely not? I pushed the rogue tooth out in front and compared its shape and form to the giant rocks passing by.

Luna was quite a way off, seemingly in a world of her own, and hadn't noticed my predicament. Maybe she was on auto-pilot and asleep. She certainly wasn't moving much. Maybe she'd already forgotten about Mars. I hoped not.

My mouth had done the right thing and formed the words, but as I shouted into this frozen waste, I couldn't hear a thing. Either I was suddenly deaf, or the mute switch of space was working as it obviously should. Shouting in a vacuum, according to science, won't work, but it didn't stop me. In my increasing panic, more of the little fuckers piled out, more teeth than a human mouth could hold.

'No need to shout, Dennis. What's up?'

Luna's indifference to my plight didn't help. It seemed to me that she was taking this far too casually, as she slowly sculled her way over to see what the hell was going on.

I'd missed colliding with the first monster-sized molar as it whizzed by, if that wasn't bad enough. And now I was paralysed, not just my mouth, but every part of my body was frozen and numb. I was trapped, trussed in ice like a mummified corpse. Inside, I could feel the dentist's probe, picking and scraping around whatever was left. Every scrape, every pick and sharp jab, went to the pit of my stomach and the vile taste of old toothpaste and pink mouthwash only added to my terror.

Screams were just futile mumblings; no-one other than Luna would hear me, however hard I tried. Like thick smog, frothing paste spewed out. Consumed by irrational fears, consciousness began to fade as another colossal incisor whizzed by. Its wicked smile taunted my deranged mind.

'This'll help!'

But before I could say 'What will?', Luna's right hand slapped my face hard.

The balloon of teeth and froth hovering in front of me exploded. I was mortified and screamed. 'I *neeeeeeeed* those!'

'No, you don't, and nor do we need you conjuring up massive molars. You're just having a wee nightmare. It happens up here sometimes, just relax and breathe deeply. All your teeth are just where they should be. Trust me, I'm an orthodontist!'

'A what?'

'Dentist, you twit!'

'Really?'

'No, you looney. Hey, we're almost there.'

I continued checking for missing teeth as the red planet loomed. Way behind, Earth felt so far away, a blue dot now out of reach. I hoped this option was as safe as she'd promised.

Luna and I stood on the surface of Mars, looking into an enormous crater. Me, the first person ever to...

'Afraid not, Dennis, this isn't your Mars, it's mine. Yours is where you left it back in your dimension.'

'Really? Oh, so, is this just like ours?'

'Yep, in every detail.'

I looked around. 'Including those footprints over there?'

Luna's eyes shot open wide as her head swept from side to side like a dog trying to find food. And then she stopped, looking at me with narrow, haunted eyes. Definitely not happy.

'April Fool!' I thought it was funny. 'Before you hit me again, I did find something.'

I pointed to the ground behind me.

Luna's clenched fist relaxed as she peered past my grin.

There in the red dust I'd quickly drawn something; a large heart with D&L written inside. I thought it would cheer her up.

Surprisingly, she said nothing and walked off.

'Where are you going now? No loungers up here.'

But as sure as dreams are dreams, I found Luna behind a large boulder, reclined on a lounger.

'Bugger me, you're good!'

'No, Dennis, once again it's you. I didn't bring this up here.'

I felt I was treading on Martian eggshells and grimaced.

'Want some Post-its?'

It sounded like I was offering a bowl of nibbles.

Luna looked up and sighed heavily. 'Huh, should do really. But you remember me saying we're safe up here because blah blah blah?'

'Yeah.'

'Well, that's not quite true. I'm really sorry, but I miscalculated. I...I can't always remember everything, particularly important stuff. So in all the commotion I'd forgotten you'd already been here in my dimension, though you won't remember. We tried out-running Reaper here before, but he still managed to find us.'

I wasn't certain where this was going but hoped for better news. It didn't come.

Luna groaned. 'When I first started, many years ago, Reaper was busy with the plague. But he was taking shortcuts, so I was sent to stop his activities. Death, at the time, was full of pointless bureaucracy and a lack of good managers didn't deter Reaper from his unlawful activities. It only encouraged him.'

I was sort of following this...but only just.

She continued, 'In my eagerness, I improved management practice and created a monitoring system which enabled us to track him and his department more readily. Much better than letting them do what they'd always done, heh? Hardly any mistakes these days, except I've forgotten one of the basic rules.'

'What's that?'

'Check antecedent data for subject similarities. How could I be so stupid and miss that we'd already been here eight times. To be honest, which I am more often than not, I might be getting past it.' Luna looked me up and down, expecting a response.

I thought I'd keep it light.

'So we haven't outrun Reaper yet. Then why don't we just go further out?'

'Without checking the data, I'm not certain that would help. You see, I've been many places over time, with quite a few abductees. I'd need to check, but the file is back in the office.'

'Can't you access it wirelessly or cast a spell or something?'

'I'm not a bloody witch, Dennis. No broom or cat here, I'm afraid. No, I've messed up.'

'So, I'm an exception then, am I, keeping you on your toes?'

A faint smile crossed her troubled face. 'You definitely are an exception, Dennis; the exception.'

'Problems are to be solved and there are bad apples wherever you go, Luna. Except, in my case, our apple is particularly rotten. But past it? You're a bloody marvel, that's what you are. Look at you, er…young-ish, slim, attractive, and strong, if your slaps are anything to go by.'

That seemed to reduce her self-doubt a smidge. 'Thank you. Unfortunately, we haven't made as much progress as we should've.'

'*Really*?'

As I looked across the barren Martian surface, it did feel like we were in a bit of a pickle, because it wouldn't be long before Reaper discovered where we'd gone.

'To be honest,' said Luna, 'I never get things right first time, it's exhausting. It's always chase after chase after chase after ch—'

'Yep, know how it feels. Remember, it's my chase. So what about other angels helping out?

'That's not how it works, it's my task. I have all the right tools to get the job done, but they're scattered about in my head rather than being neatly packaged. It's overwhelming.'

'But you must have an army of angels just flying about wanting to get stuck in? They'd beat the shit out of Reaper, I'll bet.'

Luna grinned. 'You're funny! No, we have plenty of angels but not many with front-line experience. That means they can't fly, so they work on the ground.'

'You have wings?'

'Oh, yes.'

I walked carefully around my vulnerable friend to see if…

'You can't see them, Dennis. It's a bad day when you need to use your wings.'

'Oh, okay. Sorry, but I thought they might be poking out somewhere.'

'You twit.'

'Broom?'

She giggled. 'Idiot!'

I had an idea.

'Okay, I know you need help to get your plan up and running and asking your department for help clearly isn't an option, so this is what I think. You don't have to do this alone.' I beamed for all I was worth, hoping she would twig.

But Luna looked confused and worried.

'Without conditions,' I continued, 'I want to offer my help. Which is a bit weird, me helping you to help me, but I'm good with that. Two minds are better than one, aren't they?'

Now it was time for Luna's mouth to drop open as she looked at me with clear uncertainty. At the same time though, there was a twinkle in her eye.

'Look, I won't turn my back on those things you lack, but if you can let go of the control you think you need, perhaps things needn't be perfect. Less control, less analysis and my help might give us the flexibility we need, maybe? You can be more strategic. What's the worst that could happen?'

Luna liked strategic; I knew she would. But help from the person you're rescuing clearly wasn't standard practice. Was she worried about what they would say back in the office? For all my pomp and bluster, it wouldn't just be Luna's neck on the line, but mine too. No change there, then.

Just then, Luna coughed and from of her mouth a little piece of ivory popped out and hovered in front of her puzzled face.

'That's never happened before.'

'Welcome to my world.'

And I guess that was the point, *my* world. A human seed of an idea, a mad, crazy idea, was growing more stupid with each passing moment. I looked nervously to Luna, hoping she'd not been inside my dreamy head to see what was developing in the sawdust.

So there I was, in the driver's seat made for my guardian angel and I wasn't planning to let her down. I hoped stupidity would trump the madness that followed us.

'Time for us to go, my friend, and head back to my world, my head. I know we can do this, and trust me, it's the best thing you'll ever do. I know it is. We can't fight him off in a place I don't know. We just can't.'

Together, we gazed out into this desolate yet intriguing world, over far ridges, huge gullies and massive mountains, and wished we could linger longer, in safety. But not today.

If only those in Little Glum could see me now. I grabbed a handful of red sand and let it pour slowly between my fingers. Then, without another thought, I grabbed Luna's hand.

'Ready?'

'Yes, I think so, Dennis. Let me get my notes together.'

'Ready, steady…'

'My notes, hold on a second.'

Luna stuffed wads of Post-its into her pockets.

We were losing time.

'Right, have you finished or have you a wipe board you want to take or a set of spreadsheets? Pens, pencils, sharpener perhaps. No?'

She seemed particularly uncertain about the wipe board, and gripped the sharpener like it was made of gold. Weird.

'Right, Luna, together on the count of three. One, three.'

As we streaked away at a startling speed, Luna shouted, 'What about two?'

A new me answered, 'Failing to plan is not, I repeat, is not planning to fail.'

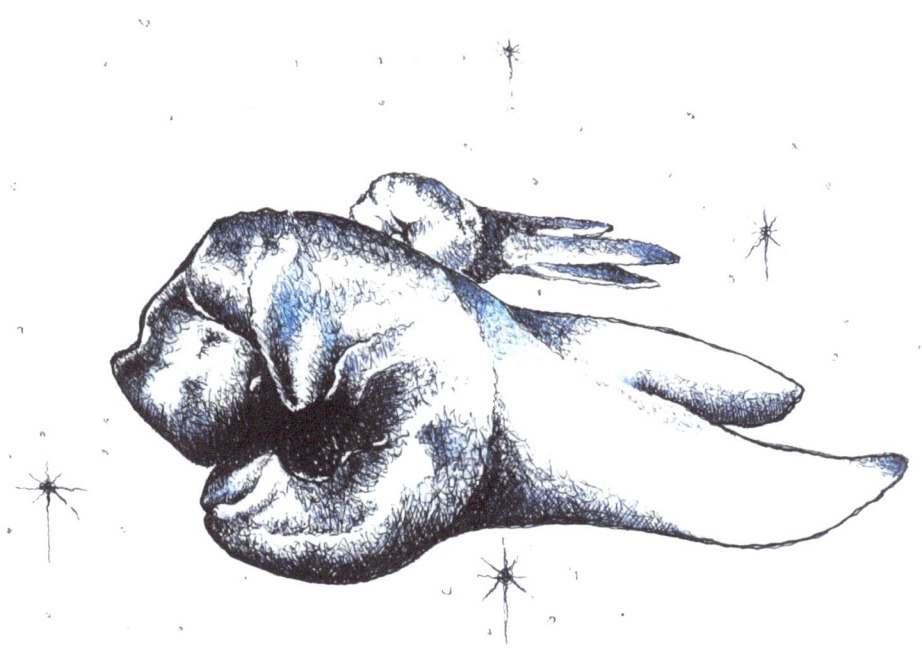

9. Heath Robinson

I was mad. What, Dennis save the day? It was the most ridiculous thing I'd ever done. I had difficulty surviving each day back home and now I had someone else to worry about. What was I thinking?

In a long, arching sweep, we hurtled toward distant Earth. As we did so, the inkiness of space far ahead to our right suddenly became extremely dark. Way off, Death's lieutenant was fast en route to the place we'd left only moments before.

I shuddered, and doubt came knocking pretty quickly on its heels. Perhaps it would have been better for everyone if I'd been taken out by the truck at the office.

But this was no time for moping. Hopefully he'd take his time searching for us. There were many nooks, crannies, and hidey holes to check if he was thorough. But, to be honest, I expected him to skim over the place rather than turn each boulder.

Time would soon tell.

Silly as it was, I chuckled, as inside, mad ideas began to gather pace.

Luna poked me in the side.

'What's up with you?'

'Nothing much.'

I don't think she liked the sound of that. She turned and looked behind, worried. She wasn't alone.

We desperately needed to hide, but in the middle of nothing, it can be tricky.

Before Reaper set down on the rocky red planet, an idea popped into my head.

Dreams, even dull dreams, always confused the hell out of me, but I'd been thinking about this for some time. Never did I think of the journey as a dream – nightmare, yes – but you know a proper dream because everything felt so real.

So that was it, the idea to use the power and purpose of dreams in this dimension, to confuse the hell out of the hunter. There was no time to discuss the matter with Luna, but it was definitely worth a go.

I closed my eyes tight, hoping to conjure up something stunning, But since when has a dream ever gone the way you'd like it to?

Clad in wooden pallets, sticky-back plastic, numerous bicycle frames and kitchen foil, my idea of escape wasn't, it seems, well thought through. Bouncing about in a flea-bitten leather chair, trying to pilot the most powerful DIY rocket ship ever, I doubted my imagination.

The fireside carriage clock wobbled precariously on the rickety wooden dashboard, suggesting we would reach Earth in three hours. That's two hours and fifty-nine minutes too long when you've a certified nightmare in the neighbourhood. But I'd wrapped us up in a cloaking device, and thereby tore through the icy void, avoiding Reaper's gaze for now at least.

Fingers crossed.

Once Luna had recovered from the shock of this insane, rickety rocket ship, she decided to mimic my lunacy with her own personal touches.

'If you can't beat 'em, join 'em,' she chirped, and of course I agreed.

A collection of potted plants, small patio area with barbecue, festoon lights and a line of kiddie beach windmills gave it a homely feel. A long string of multi-coloured kites, including the skull and crossbones, finished off the reckless display perfectly. This was a side of my partner I liked, one without a list.

Reaper was, for his part, but an element of this vast alter-dimension. His realm maybe, but he wasn't in charge of me or my subconscious; he was a cast member, and I was now the assistant producer of my own luck or demise. With the help of a rather nervous backseat passenger, it was my intention to escape death in whatever way I could.

Luna's eyes were shut tightly, and her fingers firmly crossed behind her back. To be honest, she didn't look overly happy, strapped in with a bungee, in a rickety old shed held together with six-inch nails. Equally, who'd be happy sitting on top of a gigantic homemade bomb? I wasn't planning to tell her.

'I can still hear you.'

Hmmm. Hanging down in front of me on a piece of thread were two white molars, mementos of mine and Luna's trip so far. It was stupid, I know, but so was the next part of our journey.

He searched for longer than I expected, but eventually the lounger behind the boulder gave us away. Why Luna didn't see the funny side of D&L written inside the large heart god only knows. As it turned out, she wasn't the only one.

Sound travels mightily fast in this dimension, I found out, if you're a demon, because 32,164 miles behind, we heard his savage howl loud and clear. We looked to one another and screamed, 'He's found the heart.'

I wasn't chuckling now, and realised we had to come up with something damned quick.

My bandana would have waved in the breeze if space had such a thing, but for now it wrapped around my forehead, flaps hanging limply behind. I'd hastily drawn a Union Jack on the front and, for good measure, a V sign and a number of bomb symbols like they'd painted on the side of WW2 bombers. Unfortunately, mine looked more like silhouette penises than things of mass destruction. But I was fired up and hoping to avoid oblivion, so I gritted my teeth. Speed was of the essence.

'You're going much too fast, Dennis. Slow up or we'll break up,' shouted a frantic Luna as my dream ship rattled and banged ever onward.

'Heath Robinson won't let me down, will you, old chap!'

We rammed through rocks and dust, butterflies and all sorts of creatures I hadn't expected. I knew we should have had a bigger windscreen. But as the wipers cleaned the little buggers off, pieces of my ship were peeling away like dandruff, suffering from the vibrations of the rockets strapped beneath our arses.

I was caning it to get home but also to get distance between Reaper and us. I looked into an array of chrome mirrors and so far couldn't see him nor feel his presence. But like a cold wet winter, we knew he was coming.

As it was, the tops of my trainers were parting from their soles and my wriggling toes were glowing orange and red. What did she tell me? Oh yes, not to worry, it's only cosmetic. Of course it was. This was my dream and pain hadn't bought a ticket.

We streaked across the void as the moon fast approached.

'Go around it!' yelled Luna, whose wild eyes couldn't possibly get any wider.

'No way, Jose! Fastest way between two points is a straight...'

It felt really strange hitting the moon at stupid speed but what did I care. I'd nothing to lose and felt certain a mere mortal couldn't kill his trembling partner.

It was something like hitting cold custard.

Upon exiting the other side, I discovered it tasted like custard too. Luna was covered and began digging the slop from her face. It was hard to tell whether she was laughing or crying, but spitting out jelly and custard was sacrilege.

'Ha, see, there you are, nothing to worry about. I'm in your dimension maybe but you're in my head. Yeehaaaa!'

Luna could doubt my ideas as much as she wanted, but I could see she was having a thrilling rollercoaster ride, we both were. What's not to like about diving into trifle? People would pay a small fortune to do that. Fun, if we could call it that, had been in short supply, but the happy bubble, small as it was, burst in an instant. A shiver ran through us both.

Oh fuck!

Luna was already facing rearward, looking through a massive pair of binoculars, probably technical overkill. In the distance, the twinkling stars of eons long gone were disappearing one by one. Something huge was coming up fast behind us. As disappointing as it was, it wasn't a surprise. I just hoped we'd be closer to home.

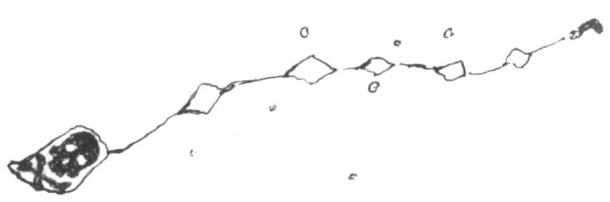

10. Bigger Fish

I took hold of Luna's binoculars, turned them around and handed them back. 'Now take a look!'

'Wow, he's much further away than I imagined.'

'Hold that thought.'

As if by magic, the demon that a few seconds before had been almost at our heels, was now indeed much further behind us. Luna looked surprised.

'That's how dream binoculars work, I thought you knew that. This might sound odd right now, but how bright is this guy?'

'What do you mean?'

'Does he do anything other than collect the souls of the dead?

'Not really. He's very good at it. Plenty of practice.'

'Sounds like you like him.'

'We were close once upon a time. He and I...'

'Don't you dare finish that sentence.'

'Dennis, not like that! It was difficult for me at the time, but he and I fell out over a death, oddly enough.'

And here was a good example of engaging mouth before brain. 'Oh yeah, who's the cat's?'

Luna bit down on my insensitivity, causing a pain so sudden, so profound and sorrowful, it burned deep inside me. Whilst she stood stony-faced with her arms tightly folded, I fought furiously for control of the wildly wobbling rocket ship as it rolled and yawed.

The pain wasn't helping. Luna banged down on her bucket seat and twanged the bungee cord hard.

'It was a young man in your world many years ago, wrongly tried by his peers for simply doing good. In that confused mix, he fell for another he could never be with.'

Luna stopped there and looked back to the dark shape, her face flushed scarlet.

I wasn't sure what to say. However, in light of my last comment, I zipped my lips. An inner rage remained between my friend and the beast that followed, that was clear; but who was the man?

'He was someone I was very fond of, if you want to know. A mortal. Reaper was jealous of my feelings for this no-one, and in his spite, brought along Death to snare the man before his time was up. Not a moment too soon, I managed to stop that travesty of justice. Though Death was pissed off, as you might expect, Reaper was livid.' Luna was almost at a whisper. 'My reckless behaviour threatened our friendship, and he made it clear I shouldn't have interfered. I couldn't turn the other way, I couldn't, Dennish, I really couldn't. It's not what I am.'

Staring into the void, Luna looked both resigned and pleased to off-load.

I was good with that, though questions were piling in.

'You said Dennish, just then.'

'Did I? Oh, erm, slip of the tongue.'

To mispronounce my name, even after our short time together, seemed very peculiar. But there were bigger fish swimming around, so I let her continue.

'Somehow he's found out about you and that means he's planning to finish this once and for all.' Luna turned and put her hand gently on my arm. 'My assignment has really dragged up the past in more ways than I want to say. Dennis, I'm actually worried what he'll do to take you from me again. His boss doesn't know or care what he's up to.'

'So I'm kind of special?'

'In more ways than you might imagine. It's the reason I have to get you back. It's either him or me.'

'You said again.'

Luna looked away, avoiding my gaze.

Dumbfounded didn't cut it.

'Clearly you don't get a say in the matter, Dennis. You never have.'

My dream, as basic as it was, stopped, like an old movie reel, paused in mid-flight, neither in heaven nor hell but somewhere in the dimension between. It stopped because she was protecting me the way she'd done before, long ago. I swallowed hard, feeling confused but equally a shit.

'Luna, I am sorry. I shouldn't have been nasty. I didn't mean it. Please forgive me.'

She didn't reply.

As we sped ever onward, my mind floated without focus, in the inky void of a silent dream. It raced here, there and back again, trying to make sense of what she'd said, whilst Luna reverted to type. The yellow Post-its found their way back onto her lap and she scribbled furiously.

'Luna, I've been thinking about what you said about this guy.'

She lifted her head and stopped writing, but her pencil continued scrawling on the Post-its.

'So why me? I don't see anything special. In fact, quite the opposite. Why were you assigned to kidnap me from the jaws of death?'

'Sorry to be blunt, but it's not what you've done so far in this life, Dennis, that's in any way remarkable or worthy of all this effort, to be fair. Please don't be disappointed.'

It was too late for that.

'You have another history, unknown to you, and sadly we have no time to go into. But again, it's what you are *going to do* that's worthy of giving you chance to fulfil that potential. Before you ask, no you won't save the planet, you don't have to. So there it is. You're more than just a footnote, you know.'

There was no doubt in my mind…I was utterly confused.

'All this effort seems so pointless if he'll get me in the end. I'm not ungrateful, but where is this story of mine going? Up till now, it's been nowhere. What's in store for me if he doesn't get me first?'

'Don't ask. Just trust in fate. You can't beat death, Dennis. Only I can. You can delay it, and for want of repeating myself—'

'That's your mission. Yeah, got it.'

11. Bang and a Burp

Not knowing whether Reaper had in fact seen us meant his fast-approaching presence was all the more worrying. Yet, WHOOSH; his shadow grumbled and growled as it rushed past.

Luna loosened her grip around my waist, and I peeled my eyes open once more as he vanished over the horizon. The cloaking device had bloody worked after all.

Feeling pretty pleased with myself, I uncrossed my fingers and happily gave him a well-deserved British two-fingered salute.

It was time to catch a bus – sort of.

Like a couple of kids by the side of the road watching traffic go by, we'd swung our legs over the solar blades of the International Space Station, hundreds of miles above Earth. Heath Robinson was tethered to it with a ball of blue knitting wool but remained shielded within its cloak of invisibility. If only the astronauts could see us sitting outside, hurtling at dizzying speed, tucking into a marvellous cream tea, watching space junk whizz past.

Every now and then we could hear distant growls and howls, whilst watching lightning storms crack off miles below.

As Reaper searched for us, the more pissed off he became, and the better the light show was below. Forget Guy Fawkes, that's just amateur night.

It is remarkable how safe you can feel, so far from the enemy, next to your best friend. But as I threw my last scone down toward the raging storm, my icy feet reminded me that we were far from home and safety. Fun it might have been up there on those blades, but he was now between me and getting my life back.

I growled.

Three sunrises later, we'd tidied up our tea things and ensured no jam or cream was left behind.

Luna fiddled about in her backpack, putting things away. 'Hey, Dennis, what do you think of this?'

I expected more food, but no. She pulled out an enormous machine gun, almost her size. Its sapphire sheen sparkled against the surrounding darkness.

'What the hell is that?' I asked with a real sense of unease as she waved the barrel back and forth.

'It's something I dreamt up to help us.'

'Why's it got a blue shimmer?'

'Battle colours.'

'Battle? I'm not a fighter; but then neither am I a lover.'

Luna punched my arm. 'Dennis, focus!'

'Okay. How's it going to help? We can't kill him.'

'No, we can't, but it may provide us enough time to get you back home. You just load it up with these little beauties.'

Luna held a large wad of yellow Post-its and loaded half a dozen into the magazine. Safety off.

Once again, I was having trouble closing my mouth. And the bullets?

She ignored my question. 'Remember,' she said, 'this gun should help misdirect our enemy. You see, on every Post-it, I've written him a little something.'

'Words? What, *bang, bang, you're dead*?'

Luna giggled. 'No, silly. It's *how* we hit him, not how hard. I'll leave it in here just in case.'

And somehow the whole gun, all nine yards of it, slipped back into the bag. 'Do you want some more tea?'

Well, for all Luna's quirky faults – and they had mounted up – she seemed for once very calm and collected, and the machine gun was more than a thought outside the box. God help us if she ever got angry.

'I can hear you!'

'Luna, I'm not certain I follow your thinking, but I do believe in you, so whatever you're planning I'll go with it. I guess if we fire enough of those little buggers into his mouth, he might at least choke to death.'

Luna was thinking tactically of course, whilst my mind had now gone completely blank. However, the tea was a brilliant idea. So there we were, on Heath Robinson, drinking tea, still tethered by a long piece of blue wool.

How delightful!

But it made me wonder. 'Can't we speak to Death?'

'No. Death doesn't speak. Well, unless you're dead. In our situation, there's no dialogue to be had.'

'What about Reaper? Can't we, and by that I mean you, appeal to his sense of fair play?'

'Nope. An Executive Order went far and wide, not long after we fell out. In light of what happened, it was felt the collaborative template for life and death wasn't working. So, out went the chubby baby with the grubby bath water; replaced by new logic and sense of *fair play*, as you put it. It was a move in the right direction, but not as far as he was concerned.'

'Oh. What happened?'

'I'm now the only one tasked to disrupt his activities, as and when they're deemed unacceptable; that's to say, illegal. If he could get away with it, he'd prematurely lop everyone's head off, whether you're good, bad, or boring. His interpretation of logic and thereby fair, is to whisk his victims prematurely to the afterlife. Being just… well, that's my role.'

'Where do unjust souls go?'

'Mostly where they should, but many just hang around, having difficulty letting gho...st. Ha, see what I did there!'

I groaned. She was becoming sharper than a sharp thing, almost human.

'Clearly you have to be dead first, which is the roughest part of all. In your case, it's been agreed that you shouldn't come to Death's door before time. You've got things to do, remember. Anyway, it is what it is.'

Before I could say 'Luna, I think we can outsmart him', the inky bubble of utter nothingness we were floating at speed in violently wobbled like jelly. We both turned as the space around us became cheerless and cold. The hot pot of tea iced over as it headed off into the ether. Peril fast approached.

'Bugger! I should have been watching. I'm sorry, I was miles away. If I don't see things in front of me, they're not there.'

I closed my eyes. 'Think, Dennis, think! What do we do?'

Within the blink of a dream, we were off again, veiled once more beneath the cloak of invisibility. Only a length of wool, knotted in a bow, remained floating behind.

Within the confines of our rocket ship, a timely reminder echoed in our worried ears. 'Mind the doors and keep your hands inside at all times.'

Ideas had begun to manifest in an odd way, pretty much as dreams do, in fact. But what would a tree be doing in space? For that matter, what would a whole forest be doing floating in space, packed in so tight that even Reaper's giant razor blade would find it impenetrable?

We weren't asking questions, nor taking chances, so Luna and I disguised ourselves as a couple of sprightly saplings, hoping he wouldn't see two little twiglets in the vastness of the trees. We melted into the thickest undergrowth as our forest family pushed forward to deny Reaper passage.

He knew full well we were there, we could hear him screech. But do you know what? It bloody worked.

Reaper pushed this way and sliced that way with his scythe to get to us, but he was struggling with my dream.

As the beast raged, smashing and cutting for all he was worth, Luna and I made a dash for it. Behind our enormous forest army, we slipped unseen toward Earth's blue atmosphere.

And then, as the thicker atmosphere approached, it came to me; re-entry and the *real* possibility of becoming a matchstick. Hmmm, not so good.

Trees with parachutes isn't something you'll see every day. Crucially, Reaper hadn't seen us head off and that part of our ruse worked well. As we dropped to Earth, I hoped there'd be more time to think, but Luna's parachute was somehow twisted and torn, and she was spinning out of control. Too many sharp twigs hadn't helped in the rigging.

'These bloody branches are rubbish,' she cried as she plummeted. 'I'm ripping this thing to shreds. *Give me my hands back*!'

Wish granted, and with that Luna's sanity and chute returned, as good as new. That was close.

'Dennis, it won't be long before he discovers we're not there. So, in this escape of ours, is there anything you'd like to share with your classmate?'

'Sarcasm doesn't help, and no, I haven't quite got there. Once we hit land or...'

As I peered below, as best as a stiff sapling can, I could only see, well, sea. Oh, bloody hell!

'Time to change!'

And at that, our wooden coffins melted away and we were riding a sleek, top-notch speed boat, big engines and all that jazz. Luna was at the helm and pushed the twin throttles forward. Off we fired like a bullet toward the horizon and distant land.

The sea was gloriously turquoise, the air salty fresh and the poor old dolphins couldn't keep up. We bounced the ocean into submission, and at the speed we were going it wouldn't be too long before…

Oomph! We smashed the sandy beachhead at speed.

Luna, so caught up in the thrill of the moment, never considered pulling back the throttles. Why would she.

High into the air we soared as the boat smashed and exploded beneath. No damage had been done, luckily, but that was close.

Yes, we were safe, no cuts or bruises, flying once more beside each other, onward. I looked to Luna to make sure she was okay. She stared back, giving me that *don't put me under pressure* look.

Then she winced. 'Sorry, but I got distracted. *That* was soooo scary!'

'Perhaps we both need to slow down a little. Better to arrive in one piece, than pieces.'

Luna nodded.

The air up high was clear and bright, but it was best to keep beneath Reaper's radar, so we bumped along the bottom of billowing white clouds, looking out for signs of trouble.

'Okay, so you know the way home, yes?' I asked.

'Once we get out of France!'

'France? Seriously?'

To be fair, I'd dragged her into my dreams, which couldn't be much fun for her, but the boat ride was kind of thrilling.

'Yep, it's all been a blast,' she said, and I noted a soupçon of sarcasm in her voice. 'Just so you know, Dennis Foster, I've never had an assignment this bloody crazy. And as tough as previous missions might have been, I've never been so scared since you started helping me. Apart from any other issues I might have, I've become so distracted I've forgotten what we're doing and where we're going. I think it's this way…but…it…may be…'

Luna was flipping out, in one of her anxiety attacks, as we hop, skipped, and jumped at speed toward nowhere. Keeping our heads and not thinking of crashing was as much as I could hope for.

'But you said everywhere leads us to where we need to go. Here, does this help?'

Luna looked at the compass with some doubt. 'What is it?'

'I thought you'd know. Weren't you in the Brownies or whatever the angel equivalent is?'

Luna responded, not with a three-fingered Brownie salute, but with two fingers. When she tossed the compass aside into thin air, I knew we were either going to crash or she'd figured it out.

'I'll give you time to figure out the best route home, and I'll try to get that arsehole off our backs. That's the best I can do, but I don't think slowing down is an option.'

She looked at me kind of puzzled. That threw me.

'Okay, so if you were in my shoes, Luna, what would you do?'

No multiple question this time, though I suspected she might add it to the original pile of unanswered questions. She didn't.

'To be honest,' she said, 'I'd do what you're doing, go out with a bang and a burp!'

As we looked to the countryside far below, we knew we needed better cover than thin air. Swooping down through wispy low clouds, the shape of a big city loomed into view.

We knew where this was. The Eiffel Tower couldn't be mistaken.

12. Memento Mori

I'd always been led to believe Paris was the romantic capital of the world. So, as we floated above the streets in the darkening night, beautiful lights wrapped the city in a wonderful necklace of radiant pearls. I looked over to Luna, glowing in the reflected wonder of it all. It smelled French, whatever that meant, but faint whisps of street food wafted high into the night air. My stomach rumbled.

All manner of birds unexpectedly invaded our cosy space, flying so close some knocked into us. Ugly crows joined in, and we knew then their agenda wasn't friendship.

'I think he's near, Luna. We need to get down into the city quickly.'

Within moments, we'd left the swarm of ill-tempered birds and were walking arm in arm along the pathways of the capital, disguised like other loving couples.

'Will this work?' Luna asked as she snuggled in close.

'I don't know, but it's worth a try, whilst we think of a way out of here.'

Luna squeezed my hand and started to skip around me like a child. What the f…

I watched her frolic in front of me and would love to have joined in, but there was a time and place, and this wasn't it.

Fear grabbed me. I froze.

Luna stopped skipping. 'What is it?' she whispered.

'He's here, somewhere. The darkness is heavier; can't you feel it?'

Luna spun on her toes and stared across into the nearby park. 'He's over there on the other side, coming this way. No point in flying, just run, Dennis!'

Luna pulled me like the first time we met, with urgency. Through narrow streets and alleyways, we ran for our lives – well, mine. Into courtyards, across busy roads, we picked our way, climbing up and up through the back streets of the city. And as we caught our breath, a bright building across the street gave me another stupid idea. Luna read my mind, yet hesitated. The idea was desperate, but so was the situation.

We ran into the deafening *Amusement de Montagne,*[8] a tired old relic of happier times. Flying past an enraged ticket collector, slot machines, and casinos, we found ourselves in a large, theatrical centre.

Into a side courtyard I dragged the ever-worried Luna, onward into the *Galerie des Glaces.*[9] There we were, surrounded by hot lights, banging carousel music and the most wonderful array of gleaming mirrors you could wish for.

This was an illusionary treasure or nightmare, depending on your perspective, and we were now trapped within it. I had faith that in the crisis we were in Luna would find a way out. She was already ahead of me, despite her doubts.

'Dennis, I'm not certain your idea will work, but it's all we have. The needs of the hunted outweigh the needs of the hunter.'

I turned, confounded. 'Where did that come from?'

Luna shrugged. 'I binge watch.'

Floor to ceiling mirrors dazzled under the brilliant canopy, and a multitude of figures danced this way and that in illusionary chaos. Disorientation rapidly set in for us both – but that was the point. Distraction.

'We may never get ourselves out of here, Dennis, let alone him. But I'm working on it.'

It was a chance we had to take and to help us make the most of this ruse, I planted my own ticket-collecting avatar into the ticket

8 Mountain Amusements
9 Hall of Mirrors

office. Both our metaphorical fingers were crossed, as my stooge watched for movement across at the park.

Out of the dark, his silhouette emerged, slowly tracking our hurried footsteps. The empty hood sniffed the night air and with each step, icy prints lingered behind. This was no fun-seeking member of the public or paying customer.

This was my first look at the enemy, and even beneath the blazing lights inside, I shivered.

This was a walking nightmare, draped in a long, ragged cloak. His scythe was his staff, which rumbled each time it struck the ground. In the gloom of his shadow, long-tormented souls howled their obedience, and those who were witness to this apparition ran off in terror.

Children neither noticed nor understood the terror their parents felt, for they were having fun. Some giggled at the stranger's fancy costume before running off laughing and shrieking into the night.

Reaper shrugged. *Memento mori,*[10] he belched.

I understood the sentiment, for I also knew life was *only* a matter of time.

Watching out for two things at once was making me feel queasy. As Reaper neared the building, we smashed our way out of the back and ran like the wind into darkened back alleys. Treacle and heart attack came to mind, not necessarily in that order.

'We must go *this* way, into the light. He hates bright lights and happy loving people; they make him nauseous.'

'Really? Now you tell me. Oh, what I'd give to see him throw up, rather than me right now.'

Reaper followed the route we'd taken, sniffing the air like a dog on heat. My avatar watched the nightmare pass the ticket office and

10 Latin: Remember you will die

into the arcade, through the gaming machines, casinos and into the theatrical centre of the building.

The initial job of spying was done, but my trusty stooge wasn't off home just yet. Reaper entered the courtyard, turned sharply, and crept expectantly into the Galerie des Glaces.

There surrounding him was the brightest mirrored arcade, I suspect, this side of Las Vegas, and for a moment or two, he recoiled from the noise, heat, and lights. Reaper moved carefully, for the lights were so intense they began to scorch his vacant form. His stomach turned over.

Yet as he smouldered, he also hesitated, sniffing the air, for the scents he'd followed for so long had changed to something new. No longer was he smelling the escapee and accomplice separately, oh no. It was now but one scent, and that *happy* combination belonged equally to my saviour and me.

Keeping the avatar's eyes on Reaper helped us create as much distance as possible. But running like hell is okay when its twenty metres; it's not okay for a lard arse like me, whose treacle legs had returned. So, holding on to a lamp post for a quick breather seemed a good idea. However, sweaty palms were no match for gravity and from a crumpled heap I looked up at Luna. There she was, not out of puff, no sweat, not even a faint glow. So much for being bloody mortal.

Getting my second wind meant it was imperative I concentrated my efforts back on the avatar. I can imagine that seeing happy, loving people might be a problem for Reaper, but knowing this angel had feelings would, I hoped, be an abomination. I suspect he'd see it as celestial bad form, contrary to his own narcissistic rules.

Nausea could be plainly heard bubbling loudly from deep within, and as he howled in discomfort, the mirrors shook uncontrollably, for his torment was hideous. I hoped he'd just fucking explode, literally guts and gore everywhere, but no.

However, now was the time and place for a little distraction.

As if by magic, there I stood, looking directly into Reaper's hood of death.

Hey presto; showtime!

13. Dark Alleyways

As we raced off once more into the night, my sweaty, unkempt avatar was about to have fun in the hall of mirrors. Who was more confused, him or me?

Confusion, however, was fleeting, for Reaper believed I was stupid enough to be within his grasp. And then, before his claws grabbed hold of me, I wasn't.

I tapped him on the shoulder. He spun around only to find me waggling my tongue, and jeering, right in the place where his head should have been.

I vanished.

'Here I am!'

Legions of self-same avatars taunted him as he lunged this way and that to grab hold of one of us. I was loving it; well, my avatars were. The more personal my taunts, the more it drove him to a frenzy. Into the *Salle des Distortions*[11] we danced as both he and I changed shape from thin to fat, tall to short and…well, you get the idea.

With all his might and speed, he tried and tried to catch me and spun around that many times, he stumbled, dizzy in his hopelessness. And then it happened – he threw up. His vomit was so vile, it dissolved all that it hit. And now he was overcome with rage.

Ooops.

---

11 Distortion Room

In the back street darkness, we continued running, scared but thrilled our plan had managed to increase the distance between us and the wholesale riot going on at the arcade. And then we knew it was over, for way behind us we felt the explosion before we heard it.

Like a razor blade, his howl cut the night air in two.

Reaper stood in the smouldering ruins of the amusement building as debris rained down around him. He sniffed the air deeply and looked to the back streets.

On with the hunt once more, he ran like fury after us, his robe billowing like vile smog through dark alleyways and byways of the city. This had fast become his most hated place.

Some distance ahead, Luna laughed as we ran on. For why, I was unsure, probably nervous excitement.

'What's so funny?' I asked.

'Your face when you looked in the mirrors. They're grey hairs, Dennis. I don't think you've realised you've put some mileage on that face of yours.'

I had no time to be sad or mad. There were more pressing things right now and though we'd managed to give him the slip, the hunt was definitely not over.

'Grey? Really?'

With age still on my mind, we hurried without care around a sharp bend. However, skidding over on wet cobbles, we crashed hand in hand into a balloon seller's stall.

We remained dazed for a moment too long.

Reaper's icy presence made its way around the corner.

The seller, Luna and I picked ourselves up. Before the Frenchman could vent his feelings upon us, I grabbed Luna's hand and jumped into our reflection on the side of a unicorn-shaped balloon bobbing about, tethered to the wrecked stall.

We dropped into the bottom to hide – or so I thought.

✧   ✧

There I was, alone in a vast locker room, an empty place with numerous rows of grey metal cabinets.

I called to Luna. Nothing, not even an echo. Where was I? And what was going on? I closed my eyes and thought of where we'd been, hoping I could transport to Luna in an instant.

But no, here I remained; why didn't it work? More importantly, where the hell was she? That's all I had on my mind, her safety; fuck my own. I didn't need an escape plan, I just needed to find her. I began to run.

Only when I caught myself in a passing window did I notice the black tuxedo and skidded to a halt.

I could hear Luna, faintly. Yes, she was shouting. At what, why? Was she in trouble?

The earpiece crackled into life and through it I heard his hideous voice: ✌'○ ⓜ□○⌘■♌ ◆□ ♌ⓜ◆ ⌧□◆, ⚐ⓜ■■⌘♦.[12]

It was clear from the tone of his cackle that he meant to make his own amusement for a while, watching me go nuts in a child's balloon. But I felt different, light years past dull. He might not have changed in all the time he'd been taking souls, but I most certainly had. I'd found anger – or rather it had found me.

Courage, from wherever it came, was enough for me to run toward Luna's faint call. Around corners, up steps and down again, I ran on and on, yet never seemed to reach the end or to find Luna. I stopped, for I now realised the truth.

Oh shit, this wasn't my dream, it was his.

Footsteps, many footsteps, were coming, and into the corridor they spilled; dark figures, one after the other, an army of Reapers. I stood ready, fists clenched. I would never make a fighter, but he didn't know that.

The fight was never ending, for as often as I'd beaten one to the ground, another hooded demon took their place. Time after time, I punched body and face as hard as I could; I pulled the heads of

12 I'm coming to get you, Dennis

these fuckers and sliced them with their own scythes, but each time another clone took their place. The onslaught was unforgiving.

This was a paralysis he'd dreamt up especially for me, one that kept me bound to this place, whilst he went in search of Luna. Without her help, I'd definitely die here in this fun-filled helium balloon. He'd have my soul, and the last squeaky laugh would be on me.

In a puff of nothing, my tormentors unexpectedly vanished, leaving me gasping and on my knees. I clasped my arse just in case.

The walls of the room were extremely thin, so much so I could make out Reaper's gigantic hood outside, peering in at me.

Slowly a face emerged from the soulless hole, one that terrified me.

Out of the sack cloth, Luna's hollow, haunted face sneered and laughed. I felt sick to my stomach, horrified that she might in fact be Reaper. That would be too much to bear.

I shook my head to clear away that wicked thought. Could she? Would she?

In my defeat, I dropped my head into my hands and, without hope, shouted the craziest nonsense into the air. ●□❖♏ ⬔□◆, ☹◆■ᴥ![13]

✧   ✧

In that moment, my heart died and to the ground I dropped, crying like a child, full of inconsolable sorrow. A firm hand gripped my shoulder. I shuddered, knowing my soul would soon be gone.

'Dennis, it's me, Luna. Get up. We need to get out of here. He's on his way.'

I wiped the tears from my eyes before looking up, but instead of Luna, Reaper loomed in front. He'd fooled me, and his wickedness couldn't care less. But I cared, and gritted my teeth.

---

13 I love you, Luna!

'Go on then, do your worst. And to think I was dull and incompetent.'

And then, from out of nowhere, I sneezed. I grabbed Reaper's sleeve and blew hard into the coarse cloth. He looked perplexed.

'That's Guardian good luck, that is. But you and I know it's snot.'

I grinned inanely. He didn't.

I'd no idea what I was going to do next. Why I'd want to antagonise him now at the end of things, I didn't know. Mind you, what better time would there be?

So I fucked and blinded like a trooper.

As I spat and cursed, there outside, behind Reaper, was Luna. How the hell?

She put her hands over her ears and motioned for me to do the same.

Reaper's claws tapped out his boredom on his long rusty blade as my ranting finally came to an end. I had neither breath nor expletives left, but it felt good to offload. This condemned man had said his last words and Reaper made ready for the end of Dennis Foster.

Finally.

Except he had no idea Luna was there as all his bitterness was focused on me, kneeling before him, shaking hands cupping my ears rather than my eyes.

I looked up and grinned like a ventriloquist.

'Gottle O'Geer, Gottle O'Geer' was all I could think of.

'⌀□□♎♌⊠♏ ☌■♎ ♑□□♎   □⧓♎♎☉■♍♍, ☞□◆◆♏□!'[14] was all I heard.

I nodded enthusiastically and pointed outside.

My eyes were half closed.

The scythe dropped.

14 Goodbye and good riddance, Foster!

✧ ✧

My head didn't part company, as I expected. The blade failed to follow through on its promise, and as I trembled in fear, it twitched hungrily, just inches from my shoulders.

Stupid curiosity made him follow the direction of my shaky finger and there through the membrane of the balloon he could see Luna grinning widely.

The scythe was poised too close for comfort, that was a given, but the point of Luna's sharp needle was already against the unicorn, primed to burst Reaper's dream. It was not a matter of nerves, just speed. Fingers twitched in this macabre spaghetti western, as the adversaries held their nerve.

For my part, I held my breath, closed my sphincter, and made a wish. This time liquorice didn't feature as an option.

BANG!

The noise was deafening, and I thought my body had torn apart. But here I was, staggering to my feet in utter disbelief. Another dream? Dead?

And then the most wondrous sound. Her voice, my Luna, clear and sassy.

'Still here then, twit.'

I jumped around and whooped for joy, whilst Luna tried explaining her absence and apologised for leaving me. Something about Post-its and hearts, delays, and other stuff too. I took in as much as my ringing ears would allow, but to be honest I couldn't have cared, for she was back.

'…and as I was saying, the Chief didn't take too kindly to being disturbed on holiday.'

'Chief. Holiday. What?'

'A couple of hundred years and she'll be back in the office. I didn't have that time to wait, so I took the chance to request…'

I wasn't listening.

Well, yes, I was, tinnitus apart, but I was dazed and confused.

'What did you ask your chief?'

'Oh, it was something I needed to ask and couldn't send a fax. I wasn't certain I'd get it. But I have, so it was well worth going. You know, she's having fun in some sulphuric ocean bar in the Andromeda galaxy. Somewhere over there.'

Luna was distracting me again.

She didn't have to, but fax? That definitely threw me. As I followed her finger into the Parisian sky, we found ourselves staring across fast-moving traffic heading to the train station.

Perhaps that was it; get on a fast train back to England. I pulled Luna hard.

Cars screeched, horns blared, and wonderful curses filled the air. Our death-defying leap was graphically recorded in tyre marks across six lanes of tarmac, but we made it in one piece – just.

Down the stairways we headed, till we reached the arrival and departure platforms and a myriad of rail tracks.

'Dennis, you make me laugh, you really do. A train, of all things? It's not a bullet train, you know, and besides it needs to get up to speed. No, we need something else.'

I used to love trains, their size, their smells; that's why we were there. Countless commuters were all heading somewhere, all except us. We were getting nowhere fast, and standing in the open, debating what type of ticket to get, was insane.

What sort of dream was that?

And then we both felt it.

The ground buckled and shuddered as Reaper howled his coming.

'Doesn't the exterminator *ever* get bored with this shit?'

It was a rhetorical question.

Luna turned and peered down the tracks. In the distance something massive was chewing up lines and smashing through sidings, carriages, and goods wagons. Up the escalators we bolted, leaping barriers and barging guards, till we reached the open street.

The phantom train below crashed at the end of the line and ploughed through terrified travellers before heading up the escalators. It smashed through the building and turned its steaming nose toward us. In what was left of the driver's cabin, a chilling hiss belched into the night air.

Reaper was once again too close for comfort.

We ran back across the wide highway; more tyre tracks, screeching, swearing and horns.

Bloody horns! Thanks for letting him know where we are.

'In here.'

I pushed Luna into one of a long line of dull grey telephone kiosks and squeezed in behind her. Not enough room to swing a cat or breathe in, but I hoped he'd not seen us.

In the shadows, we looked back at the station through the grubby glass. There he was hissing and pissing steam, the other side of the highway, as blue lights and sirens wailed toward him.

The cavalry was coming, lots of them, it seemed; great, but to do what? For starters, they didn't have cuffs his size and they'd piss him off big time if they shot him. But that was their problem.

Oh shit, no it wasn't! He'd seen us.

We scrambled at the door to run but – bugger! – it wouldn't open. We were trapped.

Reaper fired up the engine and headed toward us, through the traffic. More screeches, crashing and cursing.

Our chests heaved in panic as the engine raced into, over and through the waiting police line.

Gunshots and ricochets pierced the night air as moments

separated us from being crushed and Reaper getting his ever-evasive prize.

Luna gripped my hand and with her other, turned my cheek, gently kissing my lips.

Before I could say anything, it all went black.

14. Angle of the Dangle

What happened, I didn't know, but when the light returned, Luna's hand was cupped across her mouth. She looked mortified. Our meeting with the Angel of Death had been close, way too bloody close. She knew it, and so did I, so as she looked me in the eye, I knew there was a punchline, but didn't expect…

'I think we should take Plan B.'

'Plan B? We need a Plan B? You actually made another plan? I thought you'd got this.'

'That, if you hadn't noticed, was way too bloody close.'

'Those were my exact thoughts.' I nodded eagerly in agreement.

'Well, we can't let him get that close again, and he's not far away, I can sense it. So here's the deal. The alternative is more like A^2 rather than Plan B. I did some quick calculations.'

She fiddled with a number of Post-its. 'Yes, here it is. "The angle of the dangle is equal to the sum of money, divided by an HB pencil, multiplied by Pi."'

I had no idea where she was coming from, but I assumed anyone who studied higher level cosmic maths would know she was right.

'I know I am. I need the angle of the dangle to configure Plan A^2.'

'But…' was all I had time for.

We weren't falling like we did the first time we met. Nope, we were travelling downward in relative style, but fast, incredibly fast.

Lights flashed here and there, but it felt warm, like a summer's eve.

Then left, right, up, down across and down again before we came to a slow stop and, voila, there we were, floating in the dark middle of nowhere.

And this was Plan B – or was it A^2?

I was losing track, and I'd neither money nor HB pencil. What kind of shit would we be in if we needed Plan C?

Well, to tell the truth, Luna and I dropped off the grid, apparently falling through more alternate dimensions than I'd had hot dinners.

'You see, Dennis, Reaper won't follow because he can't. For as ancient and powerful as he is, there's actually a Reaper in every dimension, and none can travel between them. But I can. Anyhow, the Reaper covering this precinct isn't interested in us. Getting far away from my world and his dimension, for now at least, was the best Plan A^2 or B we had.'

For all her perceived hang ups, Luna had actually played a blinder, a wild card, and the joke was on him. We wouldn't hear the scream, but I knew those back home could.

'Well, Dennis, I feel better. I should have thought about this sooner, but you know me in a crisis and all that. Sorry to drag you this far from home, and we are a very long way away. But I needed time. I also thought I'd try and be like you.'

'What, idiotic?'

She punched my arm. 'No, random.'

'Really? Okay, I'll take that.'

'Here's the thing. Random is almost the opposite of dull, so that's a positive thing. But we're stuck out here for a while, while I work on stuff. Anyhow, your dreams are real for us both and they're literally what you make them. They're not random scenes, Dennis, they have a home too. And just so you know, it's out here where they're born.'

We looked through the grubby windows of our grey Parisian kiosk into a distant realm – or was it a dimension?

She must have been able to tell by my face I wasn't totally following.

Luna gripped my hand tightly.

'The kiosk is on loan. Don't worry, they'll get it back eventually, and it'll do for now; plenty of space for two. Close your eyes and think of somewhere…I don't know, somewhere *wonderful*.'

She had more faith than I had, and for anyone else this would have been easy peasy, lemon squeezy. However, finding wonder in amongst a life of…well, you *know* what, wasn't easy. I hadn't done anything or been anywhere to take my breath away. That only happened when I fainted once.

Then I remembered the glossy holiday brochure back at the office. Something about tropical seas. I closed my eyes.

My mind wandered, back and forth, back and forth, like the sea ebbing and flowing on a distant shore. Birds called and leaves rustled as my lungs drank in warm sea air. I was definitely somewhere I'd never been before, so I slowly opened my eyes.

The beach was lined with palm trees, and crystal blue waters gently rolled onto soft white sand. But filling the entire purple-blue starry sky from edge to edge were the giant wonderers of the oceans; humpbacks.

Whales with young calves moved gracefully through the star-filled void, sometimes leaping and breaching, spouting and splashing. Diving in and out of dimensions, up one moment above us, and then out of view beneath us. Each time they moved or slapped their tails, the heavens sparkled blue.

My poor old legs trembled under the wonder of it all, and even treacle came up for a look. The genius that is the dictionary contains nothing that could do this celestial spectacle justice, no bloody words whatsoever.

We just stood there, Luna and I, for what seemed an eternity. Plan Z[16] could have come and gone…we wouldn't have cared.

I looked to her, as she gazed to the heavens. There in her soft dark eyes, the Dance of the Cetaceans reflected all that was pure and good. I knew things could only get better.

And could they sing? Oh my word!

I never thought the world of dreams could be a thing, but in the following days, weeks or however long it was, Luna and I travelled with the whales far beyond the reaches of the cosmos.

She filled the yawning gaps in my mind with life and death and everything in-between.

Questions?

I still had plenty, and Luna gracefully answered them all. Yet, every now and then, I surprised her.

'It's not common knowledge,' I said, 'but during migration to Earth's warmer realm, this actual herd provides the meteor showers we get in spring and autumn. Did you know that when they tail slap, rocks in the asteroid belt hurtle off and burn up in the night sky? It's a spectacular sight back home.'

'Wow. I never knew that.'

As I dived off through the void, sniggering like a naughty kid, Luna knew she'd been had.

'Dennis…Dennis!!'

We ducked and dived in and out of time and places. We swam in unknown oceans, with creatures that hadn't been created; soared to distant galaxies and built sandcastles upon the surfaces of uninhabited planets. We rode rainbow bridges; watched pets and strange creatures head off at ease to their own spirit worlds.

As for the birth of new suns, and the end of days inside a whirling black hole, they too took my breath away, and as far as I could tell, even Luna's. Now she knew what it felt like to be a tourist.

We heard new sounds, visited old ones. Tasted food from worlds I couldn't even start to describe and took in scents that were both horrid and beautiful within the craziness of our dreams. Of course, there were new dangers; giant skulls, bloodsucking amoeba and other paralysing forces that assaulted our minds and bodies. But my little ninja was in her element, invincible, out in the far reaches of new worlds.

But whilst we traversed who knew where, I thought about Luna's inclination to go off script, or completely over focus, or do one thing, but forget the other 6 ¾ things she'd planned. It drove her nuts and I could see why.

So I thought carefully, and one day whilst resting inside the Borromean rings surrounding a Saturn-like planet, I gave her something.

'What's this?' she asked as I handed her a large envelope. 'It's not my birthday.'

'But I decided today of all days it should be.'

She loved the blank card, even though it depicted the rear end of a panto horse, and they didn't sell pens so I couldn't even put a couple of kisses inside.

Of course, they were fresh out of whale cards, but hey, it was the first she'd ever had. Inside was a large birthday badge with a girly pink unicorn in the centre, just to remind her of our time together.

She proudly pinned it to her top. And yet, I hadn't finished.

From behind my back I produced a large box full of multicoloured Post-it packs, so Luna could start to organise her thoughts better.

I explained that putting all her thoughts and options onto just one colour didn't allow her to arrange themes and priorities effectively. You should have seen the wild, excited look on her face as I outlined the concept.

'It's not to make you normal, you know. Heaven forbid. It's so you can be even more supernormal than you are!'

She nodded so enthusiastically, I thought her head might pop off. Then she was fixated on the smaller envelope I gave her next.

She turned it over and over…and shook it…and smelled it. No chocolates in there. Women are funny like that, but she was well excited. Luna held the gift card as delicately as a flower, as though somehow it might break.

It wasn't going to explode or have money inside, I told her, but she didn't care.

She looked inside and grinned in a way that only she could. Luna sniffed, wiped her nose on her sleeve, and then gave me the biggest hug.

'Why?' she asked, in amongst a flood of tears.

'Why? Are you kidding? You've given me so much. It's not much, I know, but Hippi Mirthday.'

So there it was. Luna's first birthday, sitting on dusty space rocks in the middle of three gigantic rings. The gift card of 10 Yoga Sessions for Complete Beginners and birthday cake would have to wait till we got back home, but she was fine with that.

So off we headed once more into the abyss; one working to develop Plan B – no, sorry, Plan A^2 – with a new set of multi-coloured Post-its, and me? Well, let's just say she'd given me an inner peace I'd rarely known.

Unfortunately, against Luna's better judgement, the inevitable happened. This galactic beatnik grew a goatee and a ponytail. Luna was in floods of tears the day I revealed the new look.

Catweazle? Oh, thank you!

We ran, fast, far, and wide, and over time the notion of death finally slipped from memory. It was the happiest I'd ever been and the first time the fug of old had taken a back seat.

I didn't miss it one bit.

15. A Life of Fug

Coming back from the inner core of the sun, we swept through sub-atomic particles and dived off multi-coloured comets into their frozen tails.

However, out in those depths, there were dark, ancient places, in a time before time, that even guardians were wary of.

For all our distance and Luna's brilliant navigation, out there in the farthest reaches of existence, it felt like *something* was off, you know, not quite right.

Luna, for all her amazing worth and courage, wouldn't let me go off exploring, however hard I nagged.

We both sensed it, that something there in the vacant wilderness. But as weird as it was, a cruise into the wild black yonder would have to wait for another time. It wasn't going anywhere anytime soon, was it?

That dreaded Monday morning feeling hit us both hard as the whale-song alarm burst into life, doing its damnedest to rouse us.

Work ethic? What work ethic?

Routine was long overdue, but like the wicked witch, it still beckoned with its long, bony finger. The bone-idle workers just pulled a sicky. No, of course we didn't. We made strong coffee, for heaven's sake.

'Now, Luna. Was it A^2 or B? I'm buggered if I can remember.'

Earth is *my* home, *my* history and *my* destiny. There would be no veering off or detours, except, one day on our way home, we found ourselves in a place of sepia tones, devoid of colour, and fusty like a box of old chocolates. Here was the realm of long forgotten memories, one Luna felt important enough to visit before we continued with her plan and my destiny.

As I walked the empty street of my childhood, a chill ran through my bones. It smelled fresh and homely alright, but without colour it felt lifeless. That was a worrying sign.

'Luna, where are we?' I asked cautiously, not truly wanting to know.

'Back in the village you once lived in as a child. This is where your fug started, and our journey together began.'

I didn't see the connection, too busy trying to remember anything.

Luna led me onward to a pretty cottage by a little back lane and babbling brook. It was idyllic. And there in the driveway was a family loading up the car for a day trip. A little four-year-old dressed in an oversized sweater, with tartan trousers tucked into his wellies, hopped up onto the rear seat, holding a cuddly toy rabbit. The mother fixed him and his fluffy friend securely in and brushed the soft hair from the boy's bright eyes.

'Oh, don't forget this,' she said, pinning a large birthday badge to his sweater. He giggled like four-year-olds do. As the door closed, everything was perfectly set for a lovely day out in the spring sunshine.

Leaving Luna by the gate, I strolled across and looked through the side window. There he was without a care in the world, wrapped up in the love of his mum and dad. The boy turned and smiled. Without thought, I waved. He did too.

'Mummy, who's that man?'

Neither Mum nor Dad answered but made ready to head off. As the car left the drive, I suddenly understood, the moment, the place! I turned to Luna with just one thought thumping in my stupid head. 'Stop them, stop them!'

But the movie played out in front of me, as it did once before, long ago. Frozen in fear, I could only scream for them to stop, to warn them, but they couldn't hear me. I knew in that moment there was only one end that day for this young family.

Luna came to my side and held me tightly.

The sound of screeching tyres, a sickening crash, bang, and wallop, filled the air. I knew what this was, and there was nothing I could've done to stop it. Shit!

'Out of the way!' a voice shouted from behind. The bicycle bell dinged frantically as a young girl sped by to the scene of the crash. I didn't catch her face, but I noticed a silver streak in her long dark hair. She was the midwife who'd pull the young boy from that mangled mess.

She was the one who'd saved me that day; the *only* one to be rescued. In those grey, featureless moments, my heart overflowed, desperately trying to understand. For certain, there was nothing lovely about today or this memory.

Till that moment, I'd been having fun without a care, but all of a sudden I was in urgent need of answers.

'Ask it and I shall tell you,' Luna said tenderly. As the minutes rolled sadly by, she gave me all the time, friendship, and love I needed. So there it was, the reason for a life of fug, a fug deeply hidden and forgotten. My own childhood trauma, played out in slow-mo before me.

'Can we go back to the house?' I asked softly.

Luna squeezed me gently. 'Of course, whatever you want.'

Arm in arm with my lovely companion, we walked slowly back to the pretty cottage. Standing at the end of the drive, I promised myself, I'd return to my forgotten home. Toppled on the neatly-mown lawn was a small blue-and-yellow tricycle, perfect for a young boy. With care, I propped it back up. 'I hope he'll get to ride it again.'

'I'm *sure* he will,' Luna whispered.

We looked at each other knowingly, but for different reasons. Facing an uncertain destiny and some crazy old fears, I knew Luna would be by my side, thankfully. But something niggled.

'Luna, before we get going and after all we're done, can I ask you one more question and hopefully the last?'

She knew full well it wouldn't be the last, even I could sense that.

'You might think I'm funny, but will it be dull and boring when I get back home?'

Luna chuckled and smiled warmly. 'Nothing, Dennis, will have changed when you get back, and yet everything in you has. Don't worry, destiny awaits your return. Are you ready to face down the Grim Reaper? I know I am.'

In her hand she carried a green Post-it and on it there were two bullet points:

✓ *Angle of the dangle*

✓ *Plan A^2*

When we reached the quiet back lane, the kiosk had been overrun by nature. Massive creepers, webs and old nests had taken over during our time away. By the look of it, we may have been gone years, but that was a guess. We set about cleaning it up and making it presentable for our ride home. As the door closed slowly behind, I hugged Luna, for longer than a friend might.

'What's that for, young man?'

'Hmmmm, how long have you got?'

Luna threw her arms around my neck and kissed me.

Once more we raced off through the multiverse of nowhere, re-tracing our footsteps of long ago. Fast, incredibly fast, the kiosk tore through the abyss of space and time; then down, across, down again, up, right, and then left before we came to a slow stop. Instead of being in Paris or the dark middle of nowhere, our kiosk popped up somewhere new. It now sported a red livery and as I opened the door, hoping to be somewhere close to home, a red double decker drove by over London Bridge. I was relatively happy with the outcome.

'Oh, are you now?'

'What?'

'Happy with the outcome!'

'Aren't you? You're back in charge with just a few miles to go. Isn't that great! And by the way, what was that all about, back there in the kiosk? That's the second time you've kissed me. You know your pals in the office will talk.'

Luna was thinking. 'Distractions, if you must know. If we don't it make it on this journey of ours, I just wanted you to know darkness isn't all there is at the end.'

It was profound.

To be honest, I thought she'd be angry with my impertinence, yet now we were heading back to my world, my realm, we'd changed – grown up, I guess. I suppose that's what R&R is often about, learning new stuff. Having said that, I could sense Luna was feeling at odds with her new plan and old purpose.

And, of course, the penny finally dropped. Purpose, that was it! Irrespective of her role or plan right now, she'd given me purpose, and if you're following this, that was her purpose. Of course it was!

'Oh, shut up, clever clogs!

Luna looked around, searching for something, something fast. 'Quick, follow me.'

We ran to a parking area and watched Ubers, black taxis and private hire cars rush by. I had my doubts about taking a taxi, but before I raised my hand we were sitting side-by-side in a sapphire blue Corvette convertible. With a mass of chrome and an engine with more horsepower than a Saturn 5 rocket, she'd chosen well. Luna threw herself across the centre console and hugged me. 'Let's make tracks for home, shall we.'

'Keys?'

'You don't need them. Just follow your instincts, Dennis, and hit the gas.' The wheels spun and smoke billowed as I turned left.

'No not that way, lemon head, right, turn right. Blimey. Just follow the road signs.'

This wasn't what I'd had in mind, but with Luna beside me, I was already on cloud nine. As we thundered on, the warm night blew through our hair – well hers, not mine. No feeling of dread anywhere was a good sign. Maybe he'd given up after all this time. I know I would.

As we left the bright lights of London and raced across the dark countryside, the faint line of morning slowly rolled over the horizon. It wouldn't be long before the sun popped up its happy little head, and yet I wished the drive beneath the stars would never end.

With my arm draped across her shoulders, these precious carefree moments with Luna were all I could wish for. So as I took in her radiant smile, the end of things could have been so dull, so different, so dead. But not now, and I was good with that.

16. Death and Shit

And guess who spoiled it? No, not me. I didn't think to say something silly like, *I love you*. No, it was *him* again.

'What did you say, Dennis?'

'Erm, nothing, go back to sleep.'

Luna yawned in my ear. 'I was just having 4,045 winks.'

I should have guessed the sun was coming up too quick, in the wrong bloody direction. Nevertheless, here we were, flying past the road sign to the office and my home in Little Glum. How had I not figured the irony of that name before now? Idiot.

One mile to go.

Fast approaching in my mirror was a monstrous black motorcycle, with a front wheel the size of a small planet. I had no doubt what that was intended for. Reaper was back, for fuck's sake.

Almost upon us, ready to do his worst with that bleedin' scythe of his, I couldn't go any faster, not on these country roads. Of course, he didn't care because any mistake now and I'd be his.

We were so close.

I looked down at Luna, still half asleep. There was only one thing I could do. I eased my foot off the accelerator. That brought her back to the land of the almost dead.

'Dennis, what are you doing?'

'Look behind. How the hell does he know? If I drive faster, we'll crash before I get to the office and he'll have won.'

Luna watched Reaper's front wheel obliterate the countryside as insanity drove him on.

'He's going to run us off the road or run over us.'

'It hasn't worried him before.'

'We're so close, Dennis. I can't let him do that. I won't.'

I threw the car this way and that trying to avoid that fucking tyre. As we squealed down the lane, I had control, but only just. Then my crazy Luna stood up on the seat and let rip at our pursuer. I had no idea what she said, but in the blink of a wicked eye, the bike morphed into a vast rotating tornado, the likes of which the village or even the country had never seen.

In terror and without thinking, I floored it. Poor old Luna tumbled heavily onto the back seat and nearly bounced out over the boot. The storm grew bigger and stronger, and the vortex took firm hold of the car.

The needle dropped to zero in the time it takes to gulp, throwing Luna and I crashing forward. Even the Saturn 5 engine couldn't fight against the power of this storm, and smoke billowed once more from the squealing tyres. We were now snaking backwards.

As Luna pulled herself out of the rear footwell, her scarlet face told me she'd had enough. 'Hold on,' she yelled.

But before I could say 'To what?', she launched herself off the backseat and stood defiant on the verge. Peter Pan would have been impressed as she stood brazen, with arms folded and a look that would take no quarter. Debris from all over whistled past our heads and the road began tearing up beneath us. Luna scowled.

I was petrified, especially for Luna, and I had no idea what she was doing. Nevertheless, as I looked at my protector, I wondered where on earth she got those sparkling blue boots.

'This isn't the wicked witch, Luna; this is death and shit all rolled into one,' I screamed.

The violent storm sucked the hell out of the squealing tyres as the car and I slipped slowly past her, toward the gaping mouth of the storm. In her eyes, red mist had descended like boiling lava.

'⬛ ●□❖ℳ ⬜□◆, ℳ■■⤬• ☞□◆◆ℳ□,'[15] was all I could hear, through the wild winds. I had no idea what she was shouting. But the storm front behind us definitely heard it, for it abruptly turned its enraged intentions from me to her.

In my battered head, I heard Luna's soft voice. 'I know what I'm doing. I'm good in a crisis, sometimes. Thanks for everything. Now get to the office; you know what to do.'

In those darkest of moments, I was utterly lost.

'No, Luna, nooooo!'

She turned and winked.

In her hands she carried two flaming cocktails, but those were no Molotovs. Downing our drink, for old time's sake, Luna braced herself as, far above, lightning arced with fury and its boiling fronds spat out their venom. Across Luna's neck, arms and hands, guardian symbols glowed blue beneath her skin. She was ready to do bad business.

Throwing the empty glasses aside, Luna clenched her fists. In an explosion of blue flames, and a defiant yell, she leapt up into the heart of the storm and was gone.

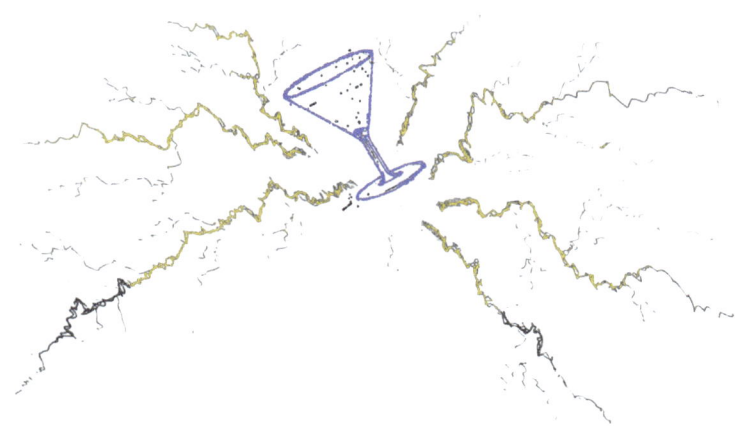

---

15 I love you, Dennis Foster

17. Eyes Wide Shut

Why I was precariously perched on top of my childhood tricycle, pedalling like fury, I don't know. I guess I'd conjured up something special and dependable – at least it was when I was a four-year-old. But now the size of an ape, it groaned under my weight. The tiny pedals squeaked as they whizzed round, trying their utmost to get me to the office before he got to me.

As the storm front veered off toward Luna, Reaper's grip loosened and I lurched forward. Now, momentarily off his radar, I heaved onward, collecting sweat like the monsoon.

High above, the most vicious tornado raged across the entire sky, with clouds billowing and buckling in a furious kaleidoscope of white, black, purples and blues. Thunder like you've never heard smashed and crashed, and sapphire lightning bolted in all directions.

In amongst hellish screeches and howls from above, all I could think of was Luna doing whatever she could, to help me start afresh.

The little trike had done its best, but now I needed to run as fast as my exhausted body would permit. Only 100 yards to go, yet how I was feeling, it might as well have been 100 miles. Adrenalin, it seemed, was on strike, the little shit.

Up ahead, the office was shrouded in darkness; the streetlight opposite cast a gentle light across the doorway. But it was daylight here.

All I had to do was cross the threshold, back to my world.

No dreams there, just a dullard, I hoped, with his finger still hovering over the off button. I knew I had to get in, turn off the computer and get out before the truck smashed through.

That was all I had to do.

Luna had assured me it would work and I trusted her.

My legs were melting, they were so tired, and my body was failing. I dropped from running to jogging, to walking within the space of a few feet. My old friend treacle came back one last time.

'Not now, for god's sake!'

Still the vast storm raged; brutish winds pounded me like a punchbag. As I clawed the ground, trying my damnedest to hold on, icy fingers gripped my body and dragged me backward.

He wasn't about to give up; the hairs on my neck and arms knew it too.

Yet faint on the fronds of those deadly winds, I heard Luna call, 'The bag. Throw me the bag!'

Bag? What bag? *The* bag, where was it? I thought she had it.

I was completely spent, just as Luna's bag fell down in front of me. And there I was, ten feet between me and the office, but still in their dimension.

I had only one chance, so I grabbed the backpack and threw it with all my remaining strength high into the maelstrom.

I was so close I could smell the bloody office, but down onto the tarmac I collapsed.

Oh god, so near.

My head weighed a ton and thumped remorselessly as the tempest squeezed the last morsels of youth from my shattered hulk. My lungs clawed for life; a life badly run, no doubt, but a life, nonetheless.

This whole fuckin' journey had been neither dull nor boring, that was for sure. But at the end, when all hope was lost, I wished I'd done something with my life. Eyes wide shut was no way to live. Now when my eyes were wide open, it was too bloody late.

The maelstrom was at its height, and all around was chaotic. God knows what Luna was doing but I sensed things weren't going well. Christ, I was going to miss her, more than I could have said, and bloody should've.

What a fool I'd been.

My breathing slowed and my eyes dimmed. This was it. I… was…finished. He'd won.

Just as Death's bitter fingers grabbed deep inside, a massive explosion ripped the storm from within, and a brilliant yellow light shone so fiercely the tarmac around me snapped, crackled and bubbled.

My chest spasmed back into life.

Rolling my exhausted body over, two tired eyes flickered back to life, and I looked up nervously.

18. A Measly Kiss

Raining down from the sky, a million – no, trillion – yellow Post-its fluttered like brimstone butterflies. The roadway, verges, houses, and streetlights were covered in those gorgeous little buggers. Coughing and spluttering, I regained my senses, yet as I peered through the paper rainfall, I could just make out a dark outline coming my way.

I shivered.

'Going to lay there all day? You've got things to do, Dennis Foster.'

An unbearable weight, once so heavy, lifted as she came into sharp focus. There was my Luna, my guardian. She'd made it to the end.

But she was limping, and that couldn't be good for an angel. Yet what took my heart into the stratosphere was a large pair of sapphire blue wings, folding behind her. That silhouette, against the dark clouds, is one I wouldn't forget, for I knew how bad it must have been for her.

Luna crouched down and pulled me forward, still catching her breath.

'One...last...thing to do...Dennis, and by the look of the sun over...there, I'd say it was time to turn off the computer and go home, wouldn't you?'

Through my pains, I grabbed her arms and pulled her to me. We both flinched. A kiss, a measly kiss, was my way of saying sorry and showing my debt of gratitude; the best an exhausted mortal could do.

'Hmmm, not bad, Dennis. But there was no need.'

Luna didn't push me away but returned the kiss heartily. As our lips parted, she pulled me carefully to my feet and, holding each other up, we staggered toward the dark threshold and my waiting world.

Standing in the last rays of sunshine, on the threshold of night at the office, I cast a glance at Luna. Her clothing was wrecked, ripped and torn, either smoking or steaming or both. Anywhere else, that look would be considered fashionable, but here her battle dress was anything but.

And now I could take it in, her face was a mess. Bruised black and blue, with a swollen eye, and a large gash swept worryingly across her shoulders. A myriad bleeding cuts peppered her arms and hands. Her wonderful braids were gone, replaced by wild, flowing locks that glowed in the twilight. There was no doubt she'd gone full distance, but her smile, tainted by blood, was still radiant.

I didn't have the heart to tell her that her face was a mess, so I opted for, 'Like what you've done with your hair!'

She let out a small chuckle, for she was still inside my head.

'What happened, Luna?'

She winced, trying to get her injured leg comfortable.

'Nothing you should worry about. He needed to be told a few home truths and it took longer than I expected. If you think I look bad, he'll definitely need stiches and something for a few broken bones. He won't be worrying us any time soon.'

After all we'd been through, I wasn't certain whether to laugh or to cry.

'Oh, and thanks for chucking me the bag. I knew it would come in handy.'

We laughed and cried, wracked in our own pain.

Luna picked up a handful of Post-its.

Now I could see what she'd loaded into her gun, all that time ago. Each note carried the outline of a heart and the scribbled letters L&D were plain to see. That's what she shot him with: the love for a mortal.

The letters could still mean Lick & Dust of course, rather than what I feared it did. I was too scared to ask.

But I felt compelled to fill my own awkward silence. 'Can I say just one thing?'

'Just *one* thing, Dennis?'

'Oh bugger off! Look, I guess we haven't much time left, you and I, and there's so much I want to tell you, to thank you for. You're my star, my saviour, abductee and know it all.'

Luna laughed out loud and put her finger to my lips. 'Shut up, Dennis Foster, you're making me blush. Can I ask you a question for a change?'

'Of course, anything.'

'When you were in the unicorn, I heard you call. Did you mean what you said?'

I didn't think in all the chaos she'd heard me and now I was cornered. She knew it, I knew it. I didn't know what to say.

The pause was a moment too long.

'Clearly you didn't. I'm sorry I asked. Now, Dennis Foster, get over there and finish what you never started. Just one last push, and it'll be over.'

And with that, she pushed me. Again.

I stumbled those last few feet.

Behind, Luna wiped a tear from her cheek. Yet again, I hadn't said what I should've and now it was too late. It was goodbye for us both, and I hadn't till this moment ever considered what that might feel like.

It felt dreadful, and now at the end it felt far too rushed. In a mind that had momentarily turned to mush, things suddenly became clear.

I drew in a deep breath. All I had to do was turn back. That was it, turn back and tell her what you think. No, you twit, what you feel!

But just coming into the village, along the yellow Post-it road, a heavy work truck was heading to the depot after a long day. Before I could run back to Luna, I recognised this long-forgotten memory. At the end, I'd run out of time to tell her what I really felt and also get to the office and finish this shit.

The young driver, asleep at the wheel, knew not what he was doing, as the truck weaved this way and that. It wasn't Reaper who'd careered into the office that night, just a guy too tired to stop. As the truck approached the last curve in the road, it was all or nothing, and I stepped across the threshold, back into the dark.

Night-time drizzle fell on me and the building as I ran at the door, expecting it to be unlocked. It wasn't. I slammed into the wood and glass with an almighty bang, bounced and lay crumpled in a heap. It felt as though I'd been kicked by a mule.

The truck entered the twilight, slipping and swerving all over the place. Within seconds it would cross the pavement and slam into the building and this time, the Dennis behind the desk would be dead. Reaper would have won.

Luna looked at me and then the truck and, with sadness in her eyes, tutted loudly. She knew what she had to do, one last time. My guardian, my battered protector, sailed over my body and through the locked door. There behind the desk, in place of my old self, she stood waiting for the truck to obliterate all that stood in its way. I scrambled to the door and hauled myself up. There she was, standing with finger poised at the off button. I banged on the glass.

'Hit the button, Luna, hit it!'

But she didn't. She just turned and smiled, the way an angel does.

The truck did what it was always going to do; it veered across the road and ploughed into the building. As the tiny room exploded, there was no hand to pull me out of harm's way this time. The blast ripped the side door from its hinges, taking me across the car park with it.

Within a ball of glass, brick and dust, darkness became a painful reality.

And that was the last I saw of Luna, the one person or angel that had any faith in stupid old me.

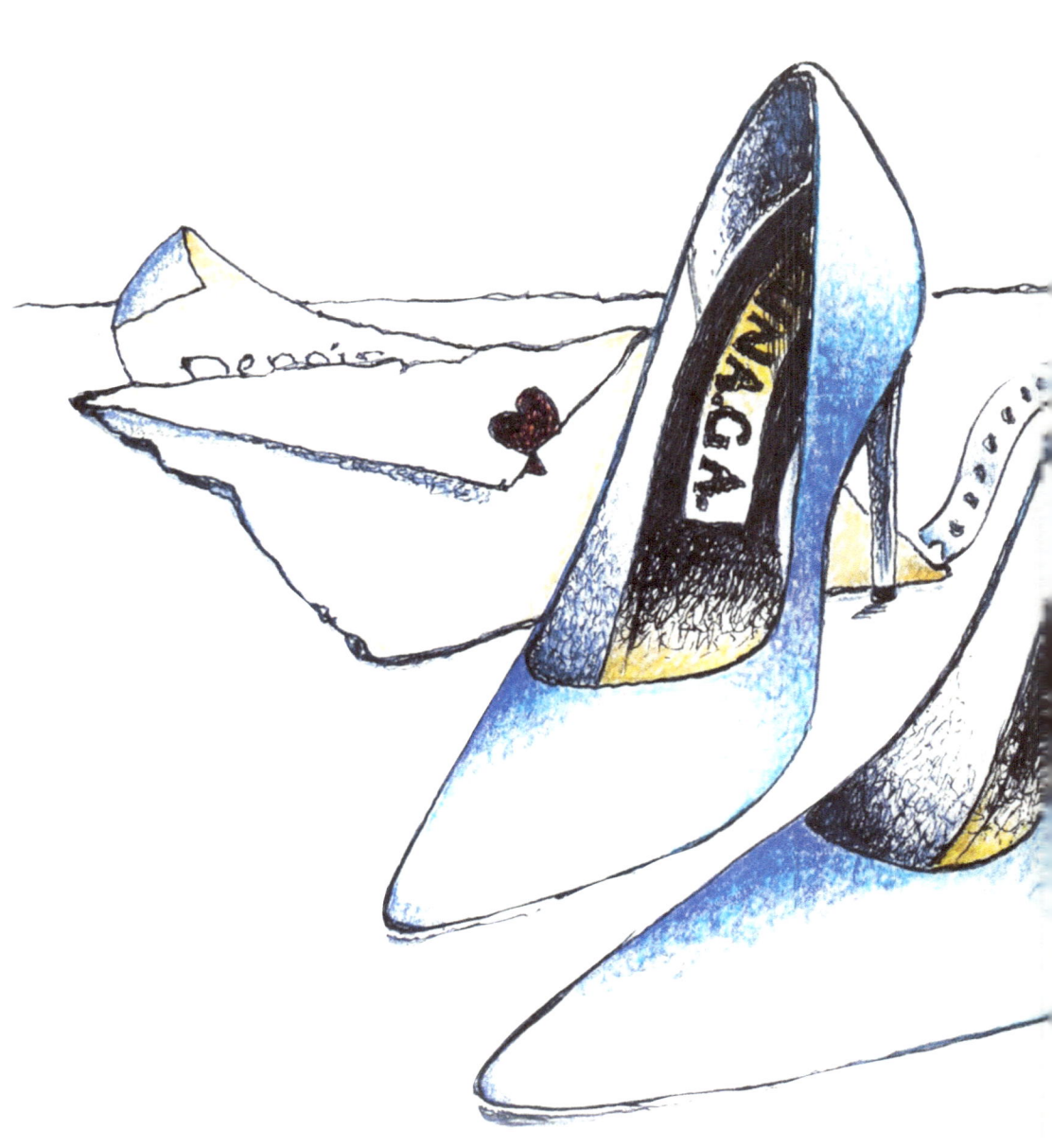

19. A Syringe of Doctors

I was unresponsive for three days after the incident, before I slowly came to. Despite the will-he-won't-he-make-it scenario, the hospital had done a great job keeping me alive.

Here I was, sore all over, yes, but clean and tidy and all wounds suitably bandaged.

As I lay there like a proverbial mummy, trying to figure out what the hell had happened, a syringe of doctors doing their rounds came into the ward, on the dot of 10.30am. It seemed I would be last.

I didn't know my eyes were bloodshot and my face bruised and swollen, but I knew they'd want to examine me. I didn't need them to tell me what a mess I was, I could feel it.

At last, I watched them approach, clipboards ready and waiting. They asked me questions, for which, in the main, I had either no recollection or went off on some delirious trip.

'Now, don't be afraid, no-one's going to hurt you. I just want to check your vision, Mr Foster.'

I turned my head and winced as the torch light flipped from one eye to the other. As my eyes recovered, I blinked through the dark spots at the examining doctor, who loomed overhead. In front of me was the face of Arnold Schwarzenegger looking at my notes, biting his lip. He leaned in and tilted my head one way and then the other.

I instinctively pulled my face away.

'Ah good, the cuts are healing well, don't you agree?' He turned to a colleague by his side, and damn if it wasn't King Charles III in a white doctor's coat. My mind went into meltdown. Was I dead? Or, worse, still living a nightmare? Apparently I needed more shots than a rhino to calm me.

In any event, they decided it was better to keep me in for further observation. To be honest, I was glad, for I couldn't face going back to a…I wanted to say dull world, but it didn't somehow feel right.

A few hours later, I returned to the land of the living and asked a young auxiliary flitting about on the ward about the morning rounds. She checked my notes.

'No, everything was normal, Mr Foster,' she said, reassuring me that my rantings were probably drug-induced hallucinations, for they had no doctors by those names working on the ward. I shook my aching head. It had felt so damn real.

'Don't I know you?' she asked, peering closely at my face. 'Nasty gash there on your cheek, though I'm sure it'll heal up nicely. Might scar.'

She took me by surprise. Scarred face?

'I'm sorry, I didn't get your name.'

She smiled but didn't respond.

'Erm, I don't think we've met before. I'm sure I would have remembered.'

'No problem. Anyway, someone left you this.'

She handed me a plain white envelope, smiled again and went on her merry way, leaving me to rest. I crashed almost instantly, yet when I came around, I still gripped the crumpled envelope.

A shaky finger sliced the top open and I looked inside.

'Fuck me!'

All heads on the ward, including the tea lady, turned and glared. I didn't care what they thought, but I sure did care about the yellow Post-it stuck inside. Carefully I pulled it out and dragged it to my chest. Those questioning eyes around me returned to their own sick needs. Good.

Fearing it would be blank, I slowly turned the note over. It wasn't. After all that I'd been through, the message made complete sense, and yet to anyone else, none at all.

It read:

ꖶ■●☒ □■♍ □◆♍••✝ꖶ□■ ●♍⤢◆, ♄♍■■ꖶ•.
❄≋ꖶ■&; ♏☺□♍⤢◆●●☒ ♌♍⤢□□♍ ☒□◆
☺■••♍□ ꖶ◆![16]

My heart exploded, causing the life support monitor to scream in panic and alarm. My eyes flooded and my lungs spasmed from the emotion that poured from deep within. I was out of control, medically all over the place, and for the next hour and a half I cried till another vat of sedation kicked in.

I didn't let go of the note.

Staff monitored me constantly. These were my angels, just when I needed them, but what they didn't realise was those tears weren't sad, just the opposite.

Four days later, after more tests and assessments, they could do no more and I was to be discharged. It seemed they no longer feared for my health nor sanity.

Neither did I.

The young auxiliary I'd met at the beginning of my stay turned up once again at the bottom of the bed. I would be her last call before she left off. As I slurped my hot tea, she told me of an old vagrant injured in a recent fight causing untold grief over in the next ward. Apparently he was an utter nightmare, hissing and spitting, insolent and rude.

'However,' she whispered behind her hand, 'he calmed right down once I told him his future.'

I was shocked.

'Can you do that?'

---

16 Only one question left, Dennis. Think carefully before you answer it!

'Hmmm, not really, but I've met his kind before. You might have heard him howling in the night; that was me telling him a few home truths.'

'Blimey. Well, it's boring in here by comparison.'

'Life's never dull or boring, Mr Foster.'

She looked with interest at my chart, and as she did so, I noticed a silver streak rippling through her braided locks. Then I saw her sparkling blue heels, which made absolutely no health and safety sense at all. I tutted in disbelief, and guessed she was heading out for a date or something equally nice.

'So,' she started, 'concussion and loss of memory?'

'So they say. But they're letting me go, so I guess my memory's fine.'

'Hmmm, maybe. You're looking so much better than you did when you first arrived. You looked like death warmed up to be honest. I see you had a bit of a meltdown a few days ago. Why was that?'

I held out the crumpled note. 'I really don't remember how I got this. I don't think you'll understand. No one will.'

The girl unravelled the note and smiled. 'It looks like a load of old gobbledegook to me, Mr Foster,' she said, handing it back.

'Huh, gobbledegook indeed. I suspect you're probably right.'

I gripped the note tight, as though my life depended on it.

'You know, there's no place like home to recover. Much better away from the likes of those grim old buggers we have here sometimes. Anyhow, I'll be off now, so be good and don't do anything I wouldn't.'

She turned, clicked her heels, and disappeared off behind the curtains. What a strange goodbye. However, within seconds, I heard her call back.

'Dennis! You've only one question left.'

It all came back like a Parisian train crash. In my medicated haste, I pulled out wires and needles, anything that would slow me down. Dragging the saline bag on its stupid stand, I clattered down the corridor after the auxiliary. Yet as quick as my battered body, trailing bandages and flapping gown would allow, I couldn't catch her.

It came as no surprise that the hospital employed no-one matching her description. I was gutted. Was I hallucinating, or had I left my mind out there in a distant galaxy? The only thing I managed to babble was, 'Do you love *me*?'

The part-time cleaner job was no more. They never rebuilt the little office, so I found myself seeking job opportunities. I realised the impotency of what I had become, in the village on the outskirts of Shit City.

Because of Luna, I now saw things very differently. She had given me another chance, and an energy I'd never felt before. In that manner, I sought out a career that would help me to help others without purpose or direction. Luna's legacy wasn't about to be wasted.

I loved my years working in and out of others' lives, giving them hope and guidance. I had no need of a compass; I knew just which direction I needed to go, and they with me. But I always had a wad of yellow Post-it notes to help me, help them, help me.

Every now and then I'd think back to those far distant heavenly places, flying, ducking and diving, rocket riding across sand, sea, and snow, and so much more. But as the years went by, little by little those flights of fancy began to wane.

I knew someday the memory of those moments in a realm beyond the stars would be gone.

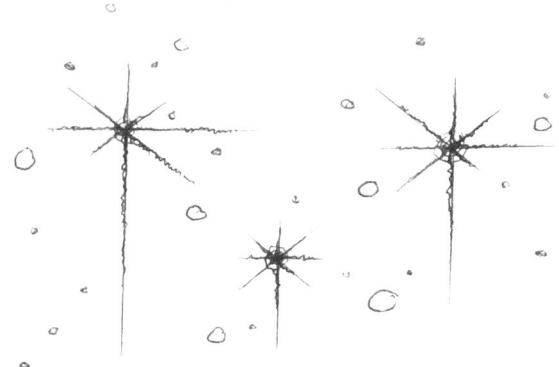

20. Now Or Never

I'd long been taking a pension, carrying on independently in an idyllic cottage by a babbling brook. I'd health troubles and scares like you do, but shook them off with medication, and the occasional cream tea. I was as active as my walking frame would permit, for old age treacle had, for a few years, made home in my legs. Nevertheless, feeling as well as any other octogenarian, I found myself in a new electrical store on the outskirts of the village.

I'd thrown the old TV out years before, having held onto certain fond memories long enough. But now, years later, I was ready to replace that collectable with one that wasn't coal-fired. TV, for all its faults, did provide me with companionship when, on rare occasions, I needed it.

While staff dealt with younger customers, they left me and the walking frame at the back of the store. I'm sure they thought I'd only popped in to keep warm. Of course, there might have been something in that, for the weather had turned unseasonably chilly that day.

The taxi waited, knowing I'd not be long, for that's what I told them. So, as youth raced around this tired old man, I checked out the aisles of flickering TV screens. All offered nonsense game shows or sports or images that weren't in focus. But there was one TV that had no picture at all and, as I carefully bent down, I could see the plug wasn't connected to the daisy chain of extension leads.

The other sets were okay, I suppose, but I liked the size and design of the one that didn't work. It reminded me of a small door on its side. I don't know why, but this was the set I wanted, so I asked if one of the staff could get it working. After a check of the connections and hitting the power switch a few times, it was clear that it wasn't going to work.

Hmmm.

The store apologised and offered me a deal on a much bigger screen, as a spotty youth wheeled the little unit to the far wall and left it like a kid standing in the stupid corner. Stuck to the screen, a purple Post-it note said all it needed: *For disposal.*

Standing in front of the forlorn little screen, I was disappointed, knowing it would have been the perfect choice for home. However, clinging to the walker, pondering an alternative, the hairs on my neck and arms began to rise.

As they lifted, I sensed something I'd long forgotten.

Dread.

In the reflection of that blank screen, I could see the entrance doors behind. The weather had suddenly turned dark and foreboding and my doddery old legs, well, they began to tremble.

Without warning, the power to the whole store cut off. TVs, lights, computers, and other displays pinged to a halt. A notable groan came from staff in the shadows, who scurried like headless chickens and then grouped to discuss options.

Thunder and lightning fought each other high above, and rain lashed down violently in deafening waves upon the store's metal roofing. No-one ventured out, but a few caught in the deluge rushed in for cover in the gloomy store. The taxi, it seemed, had buggered off, and I was now going nowhere fast.

Then the roof shook, and panel by panel, the corrugated sheeting peeled away. Light fittings high above swayed and danced like marionette puppets, until one by one they dropped and exploded on the displays. Screams rang out as staff and customers ran, petrified, towards the entrance and were lost in the storm.

There I was, forgotten, beneath a shaking and breaking store. Was I afraid?

Not really. What was the worst that could happen?

A panel high above ripped away into the maelstrom and through the hole and swirling debris, I could at last sense him. As I looked up, it seemed like only yesterday that Luna and I found each other down a similar rabbit hole.

Where had those sixty years gone?

I knew Luna would have been pleased with how things turned out. I hadn't shattered world records, invented anything, or stopped wars, but from dull beginnings I'd made the most important difference, to others. And yet, hadn't I been to Mars and swum with whales far, far from home, in dimensions and realms others could only dream of? I think we'd done okay, and right now that was good enough.

I smiled. No running this time.

But as the building began to disintegrate, I had regrets, as most people do. They were of little consequence in the great scheme of things, except one, and the Grim Reaper knew exactly what that was.

The air swirled and whorled and the tornado ripped the hell out of what was left of the store. Then I saw his outline, right where the entrance had been a minute earlier.

Tall, dishevelled, with his hood rattling in the wind. I would like to say fire flew from his fingertips, but it didn't. Yet, as he walked toward me, his robe smouldered. His scythe was dark, and the dull blade grinned with happy expectation.

I half expected Reaper to yell, Time's up, dullard, but instead…

'C'mon, you twit, it's now or never!'

It was the voice of an angel, my guardian angel. My legs no longer shook, they just buckled.

Holding on tight to the walking frame, I turned as quick as the bloody contraption would allow. There on the broken TV screen was an image of an infinity pool, two loungers and a couple of flaming cocktails. While it startled me, it threw Reaper into a rage, for he could see the image, and sensed what was about to go down.

Not if he could help it!

The last remaining section of roofing panels twisted one way and then the other, controlled by Death's eager lieutenant.

I looked up and knew his plan.

'That's brave of you,' I growled, as the shadow of Death moved forward and angled his scythe.

Suddenly, the roof panels parted from the buckling girders.

Twang!

What was I supposed to do, say a prayer?

Nah…

As the bloody roof fell down on an old man at the back of the store, two frail fingers rose to salute the enemy.

[17]

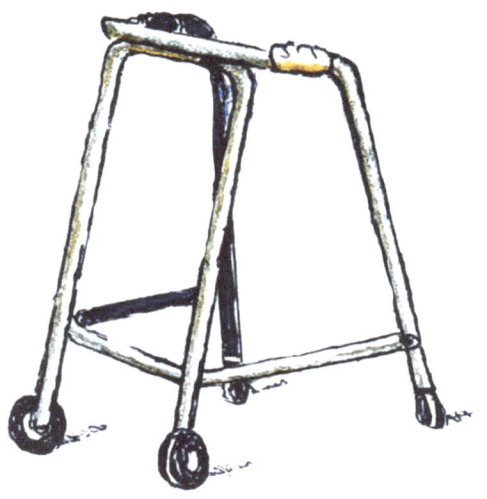

Epilogue

Dennis Foster (♆♏■■♓• ☞□•♦♏□)

The newspapers were full of the story. The monster tornado in the village of Little Glum and the loss of one of its oldest residents. Amazingly, only the electrical store had been damaged – obliterated, actually. However, staff and customers had made safe their escape.

When the emergency services arrived and searched the wreckage, they were puzzled, for the elderly gentleman at the back of the store, forgotten in the commotion, was nowhere to be found, alive or dead. His walker lay mangled and embedded in the screen of a small TV, and to this day his whereabouts remain a mystery.

Dennis Foster's eventual obituary was six pages in length, written by Jason Bourne, a young research journalist. It read like a spy novel, uncovering the eccentric history and secrets of an otherwise dutiful villager. It was said that he'd had a slow start in life and in his early twenties mysteriously disappeared from a local cleaning job.

However, some years later, he re-emerged, untouched by time but definitely changed in character. He spent years lovingly renovating an old, tumbled-down cottage and became renowned for his quirky nature, eccentric personality, and immense knowledge of all things astronomical. All who met him were captivated by his insights into life, death, and everything in between, and his cream teas were legendary.

At the Service of Remembrance, the church overflowed with well-wishers standing solemnly out into the car park and beyond. Such was the Dennis Foster effect.

The emergency services' case was eventually closed. However, for those who saw the official report, its account contained a number of anomalies relative to the destruction of the store and unexplained loss of octogenarian and bachelor, Dennis Foster.

Unresolved issues associated with the case were included for consideration by the coroner. An 'Open Verdict' was duly recorded, and the following incongruities were noted:

- Foster was in the store one moment and in the next he wasn't.

- No-one saw him leave and no body was recovered.

- In the debris, a small TV screen, smashed by Foster's walking frame, continued scrolling imagery of mountains, capital cities and astronomical sights, particularly planet Mars. It eventually stopped scrolling on an image of two empty cocktail glasses.

- The TV set was not attached to a functioning power source.

- Staff admitted putting the broken TV at the back of the store and putting a Post-it note on the screen reading 'For disposal'.

- The investigators were unable to locate the original note, but found the screen smothered in yellow Post-it notes with a roughly drawn heart and scribbled inside 'Plan C'.

- The store was destroyed, and numerous electrical fires extinguished. The usual acrid smell of smouldering destruction was absent from the site.

- Only an overwhelming smell of Parma Violets could be detected.

- No Post-its were harmed during the destruction of the store.

Luna ()

Luna was immortal, destined to aid those souls lucky to be given a second chance. The more she spent time with the people of Earth, the more her love for them grew.

Those she rescued never knew the effort she'd made to save them from the Grim Reaper's corrupt practices.

Of course, she received no medals for what she did, given it was her day job. In the case of Dennis Foster however, her fortitude and valour were regarded as the epitome of angelic sacrifice. She passed her Diploma with Distinction, yet wished Dennis could have seen her graduate on the Borromean rings of their favourite planet.

Luna became a hero to so many angels throughout Dimensions 2-98 and Realms 223-909. The 'Dennis Effect' served as *the* way to inspire a new generation of angels, who would model their own behaviours against the angst–benefit outcomes of the 'Luna Case Study'. Sparkling blue footwear was adopted as part of the official uniform of Guardian Angels.

Even with all the accolades, this strong, yet slightly haphazard, angel knew that, sixty years on, someone would have to step into the blue boots of Guardian A^2. Hard shoes to fill of course, but Luna had plans.

'They tell me Andromeda looks nice,' Luna announced, sitting astride a big black motorcycle.

As she tore off into the darkness, no-one could fail to notice the tip of her machine gun poking its nose out from her trusty backpack. It was a given the thing would be loaded.

She had but one request at her leaving do, and that was to allow her a head start before telling the Department of Death she'd retired.

On a snowy Monday morning in the Ops Centre for the Department of Fate & Destiny, a new Guardian dropped into Luna's rickety old chair and stared at the bulging in-tray. A single yellow Post-it topped off the pile of work beneath, on which was a roughly drawn heart and inside that heart, the following: 'Plan C'.

Grim Reaper (☼ ♏ ♋ ☐ ⌂)

As for the battered and broken Reaper, the world would still spin on its axis and the people upon it would still die in the numerous ways they'd always done. He'd never be out of work, and yet for his devious conduct with Dennis Foster, there were consequences.

The Department of Fate & Destiny, working with the Department of Death, created a small addendum in amongst its many laws and rules. Inside the vastness of the Dimension & Realm Statute Book, 'The Dennis Foster etc. Act' was placed. It was decreed that Reaper could, under no circumstances, harass or otherwise interfere in Dennis' life for another sixty Earth years.

Luna drafted the appropriate legal paperwork and published the entire Act for Dennis' protection on a pad of blue Post-it notes.

However, once the sixty-year cessation of hostilities ended, Dennis would be subject to Earth's life expectancy convention, i.e. dying when his time was up.

Sitting with his claws up on the table at the *Flying Crypt*, Reaper knew Dennis Foster wouldn't escape the next time they met. But what he didn't know…

Luna would be there ready and waiting.

Morals

Dennis

A helping hand might feel like a push but at least you'll be out of the bloody treacle.

Luna

To do what's right may be really scary but take that step forward.
Justice is fundamental and lies at the very heart of us all.

Reaper

Be a better version of yourself.
What's the worst that can happen?
Getting your arse kicked, that's what.

Acknowledgements/Thanks

This labour of love wasn't a solo journey, how could it be. Time spent pulling all the ingredients together, required the patience and understanding of my lovely wife, family and close friends. I am so thankful for their ongoing love, support and curiosity. I need also thank those who've helped polish those odd dreams and crazy ideas, into this, my first self-published story. They include:

- Jess Lawrence – Freelance Editor

- Ferini Media – Photography

- Rena Violet – Artistic Consultant

- Shakspeare Editorial – Typesetting and publishing

- Cameo performances by Arnold Schwarzenegger / King Charles III / Jason Bourne / Mary Poppins / Super Mario / Peter Pan / Telly Tubby / Catweazle / Charlie Chaplin

www.ingramcontent.com/pod-product-compliance
Ingram Content Group UK Ltd.
Pitfield, Milton Keynes, MK11 3LW, UK
UKHW050634020225

4405UKWH00002B/2